YOUR
  BODY
WAS
    MADE
FOR
    THIS

YOUR BODY WAS MADE FOR THIS

Debbie Bateman

RONSDALE PRESS

YOUR BODY WAS MADE FOR THIS
Copyright © 2023 Debbie Bateman

RONSDALE PRESS
125A – 1030 Denman Street, Vancouver, B.C. Canada V6G 2M6
www.ronsdalepress.com

Book Design: Julie Cochrane
Cover Design: Dorian Danielsen

Ronsdale Press wishes to thank the following for their support of its publishing program: the Canada Council for the Arts, the Government of Canada, the British Columbia Arts Council, and the Province of British Columbia through the British Columbia Book Publishing Tax Credit program.

Library and Archives Canada Cataloguing in Publication

Title: Your body was made for this / Debbie Bateman.
Names: Bateman, Debbie, author.
Description: Short stories. | Includes bibliographical references.
Identifiers: Canadiana (print) 20230501478 | Canadiana (ebook) 20230501486 | ISBN 9781553806929 (softcover) | ISBN 9781553806936 (EPUB) | ISBN 9781553806943 (PDF)
Subjects: LCGFT: Short stories.
Classification: LCC PS8603.A837 Y68 2023 | DDC C813/.6—dc23

At Ronsdale Press we are committed to protecting the environment. To this end we are working with Canopy and printers to phase out our use of paper produced from ancient forests. This book is one step towards that goal.

Printed in Canada

Secret Workings

This is not the first time Pauline has tried to leave. At seventeen, it was her father. She took what fit into her beat-up Dodge: more jeans than any girl needed, a stupendous collection of black t-shirts, everything stuffed in a green garbage bag. On the back seat, a pile of designer clothes still wearing their hangers, useless gifts she did not need and could not explain. She'd been taking the last load to the car when, from the other side of the closed kitchen door, she'd caught barely audible sobs. She'd never said bye to her mom.

And now, almost forty years later, enough time has passed for Pauline to have found a better way. Yet, there she is, packing once again for places unknown, her leather suitcase spread open on the unmade king-sized bed. She only has a few items left to pack, then vamoose. The shapeless grey slacks and squared tops that have of late been her signature, remain in the closet where they belong. Instead, she brings the loose-fitting raspberry cashmere sweater, pencil pants in black velvet, and the scarlet blazer.

The bedroom door shuts on the only home she's known. Three decades of decorating, sweeping and polishing, rearing a daughter who'd the good sense to get out already, and sharing meal after meal with Mystery Man in a smartly tailored suit. What for? The weight of the luggage tugs her clenched shoulders. The suitcase thumps over the oak stairs. From overhead, the modern pendant chandelier that took forever to find leaves nothing in shadow.

"What's that racket?" asks Oliver, a brilliant small business accountant and, by all reports, a devoted husband for many long years.

She goes down the stairs to the foyer and there he is, off to the side, in the sitting room. Cozied up in the lazy boy, he doesn't bother looking up. The newspaper conveniently shields his face. Maybe this won't be as hard as she'd imagined.

"Not two days ago, the doctor warned me I've got to learn to de-stress," he huffs, now looking at her over the tops of his glasses. "If I don't take proper care of myself, this high blood pressure is going to kill me . . . And you're not helping, Pauline."

Four, maybe five, more steps, and she'd be gone. She can almost feel the coolness of the door handle, the rush of outside air. But, no. The overstuffed suitcase slips from her hand. Landing hard, it flops onto its side.

Technically, the private, dirty little revolt started a month earlier, not that Pauline knew anything of the kind when she'd signed up for the noon-hour yoga challenge. At the Greater Foothills College where she tends to angry students every day, fitness classes are free to staff. Unlike other positions, student care representatives have regimented lunch breaks, and hers was not at noon. She'd had to ask every one of her co-workers if they'd take her slot. It was the thoughtful young guy and new employee named Raj who'd finally agreed.

All that, only to be subjected to more of the nasty weather. Rising up the escarpment on which the college roosts, bitter winds gain force over the playing field next to the rec centre. Good times, for sure. The sprint from the sandstone hall to the rec centre could rip a person's face off. Welcome to the city of Welltown during the annual freeze.

A friend suggested yoga might help with the cramps and the moods and the severe blushing at unscheduled moments and the wild fits of barely contained rage. Ah, yeah, people had noticed. Close friends, anyway.

Yoga is held in a dance studio where mirrors capture every out-of-shape moment. The participants spread their mats over the hardwood that gleams like water under a too-brilliant sun, each person on their own island.

"Listen to your body," says their instructor. Yu Yan has sleek hair dyed maroon and a petite doll of a body. But her voice is soothing. She steps precisely onto the centre of her mat, and Pauline's throat coats with an after wash of anxiety.

Thank goodness the class consists largely of women well past forty. Sure, there are a few spindly bits, but mostly women as blobby as Pauline.

First lesson: Standing Forward Bend. Arms down and knees soft. Squaring her sluggish frame, shoulders to hips, Pauline breathes in.

"Be intense, powerful and deliberate. Good. Now, start to exhale. Bending forward from the hips, lengthen your torso."

The weight of Pauline's fully-grown body shifts onto the wobbly ends of her naked toes. Great fun, this. Looking idiotic on the purple mat. For a few miserable seconds, a faceplant seems imminent. And then, in a moment of precarious balance, her ever-tight hips tear open, her generous buttocks unglue, her hamstrings rip.

"Feels good, huh?" says Yu Yan. What the heck . . . the woman's head is at her knees. How does anyone's body bend that far? At the deepest fold, Pauline gains only a fresh perspective on her crotch.

A loud throaty sigh fills the room, almost orgasmic. Well, at least Yu Yan is having a good time. "Um uhmmm. Breathe into the lengthening. Let yourself melt."

The vagina is a woman's ultimate hiding place, so moist and cavernous, filled with mucky secrets. That is, until menopause and the terrifying endless gushing menstruation. A flood of clotty, sticky mess. Like secrets getting sucked from the body.

By the time yoga begins, Pauline's been leaking old troubles so long, it's making a mess all around her. Every hour, trotting to the bathroom to apply super-plus absorbency tampons and lay down maternity napkins on the stained crotch of her white panties.

Her body holds memory in a mixture of bloody tissue and creamy mucus. There are things a girl should not know. He stunk like an angry dog, rotting meat and saliva, fur soaked in semen.

And now, there's no longer another female presence in the home for commiseration and support. For years, it was a private joke between mother and daughter, how their days coincided, how they cycled together. But a year ago, Emma flew off to another province to complete her degree in social work.

Often when bedtime lands in the empty nest, Pauline's work is not yet done. The night after the first yoga class, Oliver is waiting next to their bed, ready for sleep in jammies and socks, when Pauline arrives with clean flannel sheets. He's not a man who cares for cold feet, not his and certainly not hers. The original ice blocks, her feet have been frozen for years.

"Let's get this done." He snatches an end of the fitted sheet and wraps it over a corner, neat and tidy. The opposite corner is not nearly as exact, as if that matters.

He pauses and looks across the bed at his wife. A slight gentleness creeps briefly across his face. For a moment, a sticky spider thread of connection shivers between them.

"Oh my, have you seen the bags under your eyes? And more worry wrinkles right there around the mouth. Get some sleep, would you, dear." He fits the third corner over the mattress.

She flubs up the fourth, feeling bad, almost apologizing.

"I'm wiped," he says with an epic sigh as he fixes what she missed.

A twelve-hour workday is standard practice in the lead-up to tax time. It's not as if Pauline is unsympathetic, and there's the high blood pressure to be thinking about. His systolic reading is one point high, stage 1 hypertension they call it, a warning that his lifestyle needs to change. He has no symptoms as yet, fortunately.

"Only 15% profit last fiscal. Been thinking maybe it's time for restructuring. Hire me a couple of keeners half my age, push them hard, produce more work, get them to compete with each other, make some money. They'd work for salary, of course . . . the business stays mine. Kind of clever, wouldn't you say?"

"Uh-huh. Listen hon, I could use a bit of help. There's a reason I look tired. Crap sleeps—"

He grabs the top sheet and shakes the folds out. "Competitors have been getting away with it for years. It's my turn."

"Do you think maybe we could hire a cleaning service . . . just for a while?"

The top sheet floats down. "I don't know, honey. With Emma in university, expenses are up."

"Right, dear." It's easy for him, she thinks. He's not hauling this angry lump of soft tissue around, his reproductive elements twisting in pain while he tries to do his job, hot flashes waking him up every blessed night.

He tosses the comforter across the bed, but a fresh cramp is dragging on her uterus, crushing and squeezing, unavoidable pressure. Her side of the comforter lands in a heap on the wrong side of the bed.

"Sheesh, Pauline. Pay attention."

Her sloppy frame squares, hips to shoulders align. She

breathes in, intense and deliberate. And then with an exhale, bending from the hips, head to crotch, she keens in a long cry of agony. Yes, she lets everything out.

"What the hell is wrong with you now?" Oliver spreads the comforter all on his lonesome, smoothing his side and hers.

"Don't get me started."

Head down, he runs for cover, slipping between the flannel sheets, not another word. He folds and tucks the layers neatly under his chin.

"Wicked cramps," she announces. "Rash on the bottom. Chills from the sweats and itchiness everywhere . . . I can't stand the smell of my own self."

"For God's sake, go to the doctor then." He turns out the light and the room darkens. "If you can't do it for yourself," he adds in a sleepy voice, "do it for me."

Dr. Bertha Mission perches on a high stool next to a computer, listening and typing and reading. In the closet-sized examination room, there's barely enough space for the table on which Pauline's middle-aged cramping body lies naked underneath the blue gown.

The doctor, a young thing with a perky brunette ponytail and red-framed glasses, must imagine she's showing compassion. The lipstick she wears is a gentle flesh-like tone. "Being anemic . . ." she says, pausing for effect, "is something that can happen to a woman going through menopause."

After a blood test to confirm, the doctor gives Pauline a shot of iron in the bum. Wahoo and magnificent. It does nothing to stop the leakage and the dragging fatigue, so much for fortification.

In high school, all the boys made fun of Pauline. They were certain something was wrong with her because why else would she be so uninterested? People say everyone has a soulmate, a mirror of themselves, a fellow traveller. She hardly dated all through high school and the first years of college, and she wasn't as bothered about that as people thought she should be. Then came Oliver.

Standing on the far side of the fake wood-panelled room that day at the engagement party of a friend in the bride-to-be parents' basement, Oliver seemed as alone and out of place as she was. They'd been on opposite sides of the room for more than an hour when he sidled up to her in silence, lingering next to her, thriving, it seemed, in the absence of flirtation. Many minutes passed before he opened his mouth. He was in university, becoming the powerful accountant he is today. She was in college, taking a three-year certificate in business administration because she needed a better job than serving junk food at a burger joint in the mall.

They were the only two not dancing in sync with the three-steps-clap hustle, the only two not drinking screwdrivers or tequila sunrises. "Would you like to maybe go for a walk?" he'd asked. "It's so noisy in here, and I hate disco." They'd walked under streetlights, in no hurry. Going nowhere, they'd had a deeply pleasant, slow-moving conversation. And Pauline felt safe.

In all the months of dating, Oliver never once pushed her onto the backseat of his rusty yellow compact or the single bed he kept in the cramped room of the house he rented with four other guys. They saved sex for after the wedding. Vows, then champagne, then cake, and then trembling between the legs, her heart galumphing. She was wearing an expensive silk negligee that glimmered with silver. Surely he would sense what was wrong, she thought. He'd know there were secrets inside her stuck there.

He'd run smooth fingers down her shoulders, slipped the spaghetti strap down, kissed her neck. He'd waited patiently for a sign of passion. She'd allowed herself to moan. When he'd taken her in his arms and held her close, not pressuring, the silky negligee still between them, for a moment something almost happened. But when he made his way in, her mind slinkered off to the darkest corner of the nearby closet. He'd seemed satisfied enough in spite of that. Afterwards, he'd kissed her stilled lips and rolled onto his back and fell asleep. The sweet, comfortable numbness that washed over her skin, she'd called that love.

By week two of the yoga challenge, the dance studio is populated exclusively by women. The two men who signed up have withdrawn. Too much estrogen in the air, perhaps. Or maybe it was the grunts of middle-aged bodies finding release. Waterfall music gurgles throughout the islands on the glassy sea. It makes Pauline want to pee.

"Come onto the floor," Yu Yan insists. "On hands and knees." She places herself sideways. Ready to display the long-armed stretch into the haunches, her mustard-coloured tunic billows on her underside.

"Bring the hands forward. Tuck the toes. Good. Now lift the hips and straighten the legs."

With her ass in the air and her face down, Pauline's lips numb. This isn't a position any body wants, being turned into a dog. Blinded by obedience, forced into non-being idiot devotion, sniffing the ground.

"Keep the fingers flat to protect the wrists."

Such weak hands, helpless fingers, pressing down. And meanwhile, her delicate, not yet fully grown internal organ had been recklessly open. No more. Pauline's calves peel, and her quads plink ever so lovely, all loose and tingly. Deep in the buttocks, a new strength exerts itself, full capacity muscle actively engaged.

Finally, for once, her hands have their say. Nope, we will not flatten. Dog no more, this body's feline. With her knees down and her back up, her fingers arch like claws. Because a cat, now that's a creature who lands on its feet. It will lash out when threatened, hiss and swish out of sight, climb to the top shelf of the closet, or sleep under the bed in a nest of its own fur.

Shutting the door to her childhood home that day long ago, Pauline swore she'd never have to think of anything that happened there ever again. Certainly, she never said one word to Oliver about being bent against her will. It happened in the study, the sanctum of the house. The smells are what linger most, old paper and ink pads, lemon furniture polish and fear, coffee and cigarettes, his sweat.

She takes a sick day. Why not since she genuinely does not feel well? Look how she takes care of her husband, planning steamed fish and fresh asparagus with plain rice for supper. In the morning and early afternoon, before preparations, she spot naps around the house, sometimes on the couch, sometimes on the bed, sometimes on the floor. Curled in a fluffy ball, stretched on the side with her arms crossed languidly, flat on her belly, looking hilarious with a furry arm dangling off the edge of the couch. Purring.

At the dinner table, under the glow of candles, Oliver's face seems familiar. All this time she's thought she knows him. The overly exposed forehead, flat little lips, drooping cheeks, and lost eyes. She waits and observes, hoping to find what she's missed before.

"Long day at the computer," he says. "I'm famished." He lays the crisp white napkin over his lap, picks up his gleaming knife and fork, and digs in like nobody's business. It's astonishing, really, how he doesn't notice he's being watched.

How silly to think a small change in the position of his mouth, the amount of glimmer in his eyes, the tone of his voice, could reveal something of how he feels, whether he wants her.

"Well, then. Hope you enjoy it," she says. She turns to her own plate. Simple flavours, everyone knows, are always best. The freshness of the halibut, the nuttiness of the asparagus, how much this will help Oliver. The least he might do is say thank you.

A cat's needs are simple: eat some, sleep some, play. A feline presence in the home doesn't ask for endless devotion, only a few pats on the head and the freedom to saunter around swatting at things.

While he brushes his teeth, she strips the bed and lays down a towel, then she prepares herself. Poor Oliver enters their bedroom to find this woman standing naked and unapologetic, all her stretch marks and sagging showing.

"Doctors call it the silent killer. Did you know *that*?" Eyes to the carpet, his weak chin trembles. "Any day, I could have a heart attack or a stroke. Don't you care?"

"I want sex," she says, shocked at the simplicity of it. A few strokes, some warmth, a kind lap to sit upon. "It's been over a year," she adds. "Did you know that?"

He looks at the towel, glances sideways at her nakedness. "But aren't you menstruating?"

"We can shower after." She reaches for his hand and clasps it firmly. It's shocking how his fingers are the same size as hers, and the way his hand shakes.

"Please, no. I'd rather not." There's a bathrobe hanging on the inside of the closet door. He retrieves it for her, turning away as she covers herself. "Let's wait till you're clean."

For a while, on an island, Pauline floats safely disconnected from others. There's only the mat and her body and movement. If only they didn't cover the walls in mirrors. Those stupid mirrors. Partway through the practice, she catches this red-faced woman with a stringy neck and grey hair smeared to her sweaty forehead. No wonder Oliver lost interest, she thinks. Look at me.

When Yu Yan tells everybody to lie prone, Pauline is pleased to be squishing that face into the stinky mat, to be flattening those floppy breasts, to briefly use her back as a shield.

"Stretch your legs down. Press the tops of your feet into the mat."

A gift from her most private region, Pauline does not see it coming. That moment when the cruel knot in each of her hips uncoils. *Twang*, there it goes. *Zzzz rip*, that's another. Like a belt across each side of her groin, such a wonder the pyriformis muscles. They can be a deep source of trapped pain, especially for women. But her spine, it stretches good and long, and the clenching releases. She slithers forward. Heck, yeah. Her feet bend backwards in joy.

"Palms down. Bend your elbows close to the sides. Good. Use your back muscles to lift your chest."

Rising now, rising. Bending her spine backwards. Who knew that felt so good? Her rib cage swells. Her heart is exposed, and she does not want to hide it. Head floaty high, puffed up with bravery, flaring. A hiss leaves her lips.

Her body may have tried escaping at seventeen, but it's not freed until fifty-five. In the last days of the yoga challenge, all the secrets have been washed out. The sticky clots, the mucus and blood, have been dredged from her womb.

With a sigh of relief, she tells Dr. Bertha Mission the good news during her next check-up. The endless period has ended, and Pauline sees now with startling clarity. All the times she felt alone, the times Oliver went to sleep, the times she did not orgasm. Oliver also played a part. It was not all her body's doing.

"It hurts," she tells the doctor. "Especially when we have sex."

"Try lubricant."

The woman with a stethoscope around her neck is not trying to understand. Specialized gels soften only the edges. If her vagina was Pauline's age, she'd know. At best, gels delay the suffering, making the pain worse because it comes after a fleeting moment of hope when the body believes it will not be torn. A would-be power is gone, leaving wet cheeks, a runny nose and trembling lips. Pauline's face leaks silence.

Passing a box of tissues, Dr. Bertha Mission pats Pauline's shoulder and prescribes anti-depressants.

The secrets are gone, but Pauline's body is not empty. Every version of herself is carried inside: the pure girl with bruised inner thighs, the new wife having sex for the first time and feeling nothing, the red-faced, done-with-it woman of a certain age wanting more. She of the mighty spine bending backwards. Let's wait till you're clean. Cheek smeared over cold wood, a dimly lit study, the swirly grain of a mahogany desk, the fat fingers in tender hair. What you need is anti-depressants. There's no shame in needing help.

The vagina is dry. So Pauline buys moisturizer, not lubricant, a balm to be delivered with warm hands, soothing. Research on the internet reveals a good choice. They stock it at the local drug store, no need for a prescription.

Her body glides through its days now, gladness wetting its moments. The glow, the smirk, the languid way she moves. People at work must think she's having an affair. Yet none of it involves anyone else. Yoga, moisture—this is all her doing.

In the darkest caverns, rough patches smooth with newly

found moisture. Sliding through the cracks, oozing in the holes, a slippery awakening of delightful surprises. It's a secret a body shares only with itself.

Oliver gets home from work to find Pauline shirtless at the stove, stirring a pot of spaghetti sauce, her bra glowing, her chest shining with a fresh coating of perspiration. When she offers him a cheek for a welcome home kiss, he leans forward and pecks her damp skin, afraid, it seems, to get too close.

"How's your day?" she says. The sauce sputters on the stove.

"The blood pressure has stopped climbing." He gets a cold glass of water from the fridge. "There's that to be grateful for. Still stage one, but not any worse." He slugs back the water and sets the empty glass on the counter. "Hired two guys this morning. Pretty decent accountants. Hope it works out."

His hand touches her shoulder. Maybe he's thinking it's an act of kindness, that she'll thank him for his thoughtfulness. "Oh my God, Pauline. You're covered in sweat. And aren't you afraid you'll burn yourself?" He takes the wooden spoon from her hand. "Here, let me watch the stove while you go upstairs and change."

"No, thanks." She snatches the spoon from his hand. With her lavish hip, she shoves him out of her way. "I'm fine where I am." In all the years together, has he ever seen her body? He makes love under the covers, quickly with eyes drawn and lights out. Why did she never think of this before? "Go read the paper or something," she says, almost feeling sorry for him. "I'll call you when it's ready. Dinner won't be long."

The yoga challenge finishes with a review of foundational poses. The dedicated group remaining knows all the names. It's a belief system that lives in the flesh, something Pauline could never have understood before.

Lubricated, her joints loosen, her back remains pliant and adjustable. Such a miracle, the human spine, vertebra upon vertebra upon vertebra.

"Stand with your ankles under the hip bones. Lift and spread the toes. Balance the weight between the four corners of each foot."

Pauline's body moves through the pose with power unknown a month earlier. She remembers the tipsy toes and the feeling she might tumble. Her body is alive now, intricate and interwoven. Tectonic plates capable of shifting. She is made of oceanic and continental crust. Large faults mark her edges.

"Reach the tailbone down. Widen your shoulder blades. No rush. Listen to your body."

Each toe is a steadying point, separate from the others, grasping its own spot on the mat. Her body sways as bodies will.

"Open the hands. Reach the fingertips to the floor. You are a mountain."

At the bottom of the stairs she'd worked so hard to get down, Pauline stands next to her flopped-over suitcase. She watches Oliver in the lazy boy, takes note of his conservative blue suit and his loosened tie.

The recliner has pushed him forward, the way recliners do

when they begin to contract. His lap is empty now. The newspaper is splayed on the floor. Finally, he is looking at her.

"You're not helping, Pauline."

His words slam about in her brain as she observes him coming to terms. He takes in the facts slowly . . . the fallen suitcase still within her reach, her shoes, her purse, the thick front door. She is shocked to see his cleanly shaven face getting mangled by strong feelings. His forehead, how it creases into deep fragmented lines. Now contorted, his eyebrows no longer match. And the dull line of his dead mouth. It almost makes her want to cry.

She takes a fragile step towards him. But when she moves closer, he pulls back and she stops. He watches her with squinting eyes and shakes his head. And then, his face hardens.

"What's going on, Pauline?" He leans in. "Another hot flash?" His mouth gets small. "Oh, honey," he says. "It's hormones."

The heat builds, prickly on her chest, a tightness in her face. She's a grown woman, and her body will not be pacified. Pure hot rage flares in her flushed-out womb. She will not be bent over and made to quiver with fear. She will not be disappeared.

"Didn't that doctor do anything to help?" He sways his head, no longer looking at her. There's a fist pressed to his heart.

"We're not in love." Her toes spread, the weight balances over each foot. Her ankles align under her hip bones. "And I don't want to be married to you anymore. Sorry."

"Well, isn't that nice." Tension is building in his legs, and the way he leans forward in his chair, it seems any minute he might spring.

With trembling hands, she grips the handle of her suitcase.

"Where will you go?" He pushes his glasses up his nose and straightens his shoulders. His chest puffs a little, she notices.

The weight of the suitcase and the pressure of inertia put her briefly off balance. He knows how much she loves this house. But she breathes in and her head lifts and her tailbone reaches down. And she faces not the front door, but the oak stairwell lit by the modern chandelier that took forever to find.

"No," she says. Shifting strong, her feet are intricate. The muscles and bones and tendons are interwoven. She is a mountain. "I think . . ." The hot flash has already begun to subside. A rush of cool air washes her face. "You should be the one to go."

With those words, she steps tenderly inward towards her true home. She is made of oceanic and continental crust. Large faults mark her edges. In spite of the weight tugging her right side, the overstuffed suitcase, she keeps her balance.

The Art
of the Scarf

Most of her friends have worn scarves for years, thin silks in deep red and purple, thick cottons in turquoise, multi-layered weaves of wool in rust and brown. They roll lush textures into elegant shapes, letting their scarves hang in loose ties or coiling them around their necks.

Helena has a lot to learn about the art of the scarf. Until recently, she'd only ever worn one under a winter coat to buffer against the cold, nothing so precious it couldn't be stuffed into an empty sleeve for safekeeping. Yet, recently, she spent an entire afternoon in boutiques, wrapping and unwrapping gossamer veils over her shivery skin.

The day she has sex with Richard for the first time, she's wearing an apricot chiffon with touches of white and turquoise. After she takes off her winter coat, the delicate fabric remains swooped over her breasts. When she joins him at the coffee counter, it billows between them.

They'd slipped away in the middle of the workday. As a diversion tactic, they'd decided to go for coffee afterwards. Now anyone who happens to see them will think that's all they've done, or so Helena tells herself. Except that the huff of the espresso maker, the froth of the milk, and the dark enticing scent of coffee remind her this is not something they should be doing. She's sure people can tell from the blush on her cheeks, the heat shimmering over her skin. When the barista asks her what she wants, she wonders, does he guess?

Richard is Dean of the School of Business, and an object of interest to many, especially since he became single. The guy's ten years younger than she is. If anyone had told her this would happen, she'd never have believed them. The man is her boss.

And it's not like she doesn't love her husband. Making sandwiches, washing the car, putting away the high-heeled shoes she kicks off when she comes through their door, buying her flowers . . . on any given day, Jake does countless things for her. She ought to be more grateful.

In a quiet corner of the coffee shop with a bookshelf on one side, a potted palm on the other, away from curious onlookers, Helena leans closer. Richard sips his coffee. A lock of sandy blond escapes onto his forehead. He keeps his bad-boy long hair smoothed back and fastened in a neat ponytail. Few middle-aged men can pull off the look. It's the serious intellectual glasses, thinks Helena, or maybe how smart he is.

She pinches the paper tag and pulls the tea bag out of her mug.

Taking a sip, she looks up. She notices Richard's attention rising to her face and knows where he's been looking. The salmon-coloured sweater she's wearing fits well. The colour makes her cheeks look flushed, her lips fuller, and she's fairly certain it makes her look younger. Under the froth of the apricot scarf, the V of her sweater dips to reveal a hint of cleavage.

A grin widens under Richard's closely trimmed moustache. He leans across the small bistro table and strokes the scarf she rewrapped around her neck after they'd had sex. "What's this?" he asks, gently tugging a loose end.

"It's simply for style," she lies.

When Helena discovered silver streaks on the innermost layer of the hair framing her face, she bravely changed her style, rolling back the waves, bringing the underside into full view. The highlights added drama to her temples. It was a delicate balance, only made possible by the majority of black still in her hair.

The first time she found a grey curl between her legs, she wanted to believe it was something else, a loose thread or a stray hair from their cat, Lily. She never expected the silver to spread to the private regions. Only the possibility of proving herself wrong gave her the courage to find out for sure. She nipped the grey curl between her finger and thumb and yanked. Tears prickled and she despaired for the next time she'd have to up-root evidence of fading pigment.

Not one for injections or skin peels, she did take fastidious care of her complexion. She moisturized morning and night, dabbing cream over the entire face and neck, bound to a strict regime of self-care. She seemed to be aging more slowly than her colleagues and friends, so when she noticed a loss of tension in intimate places, she denied what she saw.

She and Jake were driving to the Sunday afternoon symphony in a rush because it'd taken her extra long to make herself presentable. A wise woman knows less makeup is more, and she'd had to remove some. When she'd flipped the sun visor and opened the tiny mirror, she'd only wanted to make sure there weren't lipstick smudges on her teeth, but her attention lowered and that was when she saw. Her once silken breasts were puckered and slack, the flesh like worn-out balloons, blown up and emptied too many times.

"Oh, babe, you look great," said Jake, catching her peering into the mirror. The winter roads in Welltown are most treacherous when they look clear. Black ice can skid car wheels off-track and cause accidents on any road. Tribute Drive is one of the worst, what with converging traffic and cars travelling too fast.

"Please, would you just drive?" She leaned towards the side window and watched Victorian houses pass from view. Then, she lifted her collar. As the wool itched her neck, she thought how much better it would've been to have worn a scarf.

She remembers the day she met Jake. She'd been the envy of all the young women. It was the summer after grade 12. She'd lost ten pounds and gotten a perm.

The youth group held a car wash at the local community

centre to raise funds for burn victims. It was one of those summer days when a person can see waves of heat lofting off the concrete and asphalt. She'd forgotten sunscreen and could feel the burn at the back of her neck and arms. She'd been amongst the last to stop working and head to the local convenience store for a popsicle and shade.

Jake also stayed out of the crowd, quietly getting things done, offering service. They worked on the final car together. The warmth of his slightly crooked smile as he glanced over the hood of the station wagon they'd covered in soap made her feel he was asking permission. The right side of his upper lip swelled over a tiny scar from a motorcycle accident. She'd swooned in a prolonged yes at the unspoken invitation, hoping he'd find a reason to touch her.

Later, the volunteers gathered for a dance at the community hall. Ignoring the sunburn, she'd put on a pretty sundress, perfect for her in a pattern of lavender flowers with a fitted bodice laced at the back and a flowy skirt. The deejay served disco. Local wives donated date squares and jam drops to go with the raspberry punch. The fire hall was on the same street. As Helena later came to know, women love feeding firefighters. Sugar is how they flirt.

The music started, and young men began inviting young women to dance. Amongst the large number of males, only four were firefighters. When Jake arrived, Helena waved shyly, then acted unaware of his presence as he made his way across the crowded dance floor. When he stopped in front of her, all the young women drooled. He was decked out in his "Number

Two" uniform with the crisp navy trousers and short-sleeved shirt that had his name embroidered in gold above the right pocket. He reached for her hand, holding the fingers delicately, and asked if he might have the honour. She could not believe the gallantry. Such behaviour was out of style. Four years later, they married.

They'd bought a small home in River Hill in the old days before prices skyrocketed. Mark and Jenny had grown up in the same neighbourhood their whole childhood. Helena and Jake had saved hard for their kids' education. They put Mark through law school. He's a public defender now, giving himself to a life of service like his father. Jenny is in her practicum year as a nurse. She wants to specialize in treatment and therapy for burn survivors.

Helena would be the first person to admit she and Jake built themselves a sweet life. Decades have passed since his mistake, and they made peace long ago. They both understand what happened. Women throw themselves at firefighters. It's an occupational hazard, every bit as risky as the smoke and the post-traumatic stress and the crazy drivers who crash into emergency vehicles blocking accident scenes. The anchor for the local TV news with her big hair and shoulder pads had not been the only woman interested in Jake.

He'd rescued a nine-year-old girl from the upper floor of her home. Smoke billowing from the opposite side of the house, he'd climbed over the garage roof and in through the window. The TV station showed clips of him coming down the ladder with the girl pressed to the ladder in front of him, held safe by his body. They took more shots later of Jake next to a shiny red fire engine.

People need heroes, Helena knows, but she'd hated the way the anchor looked at her husband when she pressed the microphone to his lips. Although the public information officer was at his side, the anchor preferred talking to Jake. He was still in duty gear, the front of his jacket unzipped, his helmet and Nomex hood already set aside, his brush cut glistening with sweat, that slightly crooked smile.

The next time the anchor saw Jake was in a bar. He was out with the crew on a day off. The anchor bought him a drink and begged him to recall every detail of the rescue. Helena can well imagine the high dose of attention. Jake loved to be of service. In those days, she was busy raising their children. She did not have time to massage his ego, and she expected him to focus on juice boxes and diapers.

Instead, he had sex with the anchor in the backseat of her SUV in the parking lot outside the bar. Helena knows the particulars because she forced him to tell her. It only happened once, or so he said. Over the years, she'd learned to let go of the arguments, and she'd accepted his version, and they'd gone on to have a lifetime together.

On that cold winter morning some twenty-five years earlier, the sun streaked the sky with orange fire. He'd come home from the night shift and shared the shame he'd kept to himself for five days. Before he spoke, Helena was glad to see him, as she always was when he returned home safely. The Welltown

Fire Department had lost a firefighter only a month earlier.

Jenny had been nursed and was asleep in her crib. Mark was watching cartoons. She thought maybe she'd snuggle under the quilt with her handsome husband. She was desperate for a nap.

But the way he sat at the edge of the bed, his shoulders clenched and his back to her, she knew it was bad. "I had sex with somebody else," he blurted. "Nobody important. It was a mistake. I was drunk."

The nervous system is pre-programmed for our survival. The brain, the spinal cord, the complex network of interwoven cables prevent catastrophic failure in moments of acute trauma. They shut down all but the most vital organs that pump blood, process oxygen, and execute life-saving brain function.

Helena felt nothing as her subdued brain failed to construe meaning. The heap of dirty clothes on the bedroom floor, the t-shirts dampened with breast milk, the pants stained with spit-up, the pregnant woman panties she still liked to wear. And her breasts, recently drained, the translucent skin and blue veins, the rose-dust of collapsed areolas announcing their functions.

He'd been naked with another woman. He'd held her by the hips. He'd kissed her, smelled her, tasted her, entered her.

"I'll never do it again, I swear." He could not even turn to face her. His shoulders were shaking like maybe he was crying. "Please say you can forgive me."

Bodies flow throughout the campus from before sunrise to after sunset. Young people and not so young, with messy hair and untied shoelaces, come and go at the turning of the hour carrying backpacks and paper cups of hot coffee. Richard's office is part of a small hub set aside for positions important enough to merit extra space and an office door.

Helena and Richard spend a lot of time alone, too much if anyone's noticing. It takes a lot of concentration to pull together a proposal for the international business degree specialization, so they tell everyone, and partly it's true. At first, Richard only steals a look when Helena is busy jotting down his thoughts and wishes. She feels the shiver of his eyes on her chest. Soon, he doesn't bother concealing his interest. His gaze skips over her face, slips below warm and silky, while he pretends to explain something they've already discussed.

Call it a trick of lighting or the perfect use of camouflage; it doesn't matter which. Helena knows that, at her age, if she doesn't enjoy the attention, she may never get another chance.

Everybody knows Richard's story, how his wife left him for another woman. Such goings-on are hard to hide when everyone involved works at the same place.

When he sends an invite to Helena's calendar marked private, she accepts with the flick of a finger and blushes. She will not let him know she feels him approaching. She'll pretend she does not want to dance. She'll act surprised when he asks her.

They take the same car, slipping away late morning when students living in his building are likely to be gone. She checks the street before going into the apartment. They use the back stairway to further reduce the risk of being observed. All of this is exciting, growing more so by the minute. He's in open pursuit as she leads the way, hammering up the stairs until she's breathless. By the time they reach his floor, they're both giggling.

In the hallway, the chase is still on. She is giddy with it, the anticipation of being caught, the fun of feeling his hot breath at the back of her neck. He unlocks his apartment with shaking hands and they slip into the private world. He might dress like a middle-aged man, but he lives in a teenager's apartment. A cheap coffee table you might buy at a low-end department store and a sofa that should've been retired ages ago. Nothing on the walls. A bean bag, no less, where a dining table should be. Dirty dishes on the floor.

Helena perches demurely on the edge of the bed, watching him undress shyly out of the corner of her eyes. A woman her age, by now, must've had sex thousands and thousands of times, yet, she feels awkward as a teenager, terrified of her urgent need to be touched, the blind hunger of her skin, how much she wants to kiss him. Around the base of her spine, where she splits in two, living things begin to turn and stretch and wiggle.

He unwinds the frothy scarf, peels off her salmon sweater, unfastens the bra and lets it drop onto her lap while he warms the exposed breasts. The complex network is fully activated, humming and twirling, the whole nervous system buzzing with messages. She'd thought some of this was damaged beyond repair, and yet, see—everything works.

The bad-boy ponytail, it's like making love with a young man. Before they begin, his arms straight, rising above her, Richard looks into her face. She closes her eyes.

Most of the women she knows had lovers while they were young, before settling down. Until Richard, she'd only ever been with her husband. She tells herself it was a mistake, yet understandable that she'd been curious. Besides, honestly, she hadn't done anything Jake had not done to her. In a way, it brings their relationship back into balance.

After she's been with Richard, she feels more generous towards Jake. She gives him frequent back rubs, seafood suppers, his favourite beer chilled in the fridge and hand-delivered. Jake has always had his charms, the strong jaw and prominent cheekbones, that imperfect smile. No wonder women swoon for him. She falls herself, years after she thought she'd never risk it again.

When he kisses her neck, she leans into him and moans. Her skin is alive to his touch. They both notice the difference and silently agree to keep it a sweet little secret, exchanged sometimes in public with a heated glance. It is nobody else's business.

Sometimes late at night when she should be sleeping, the recent encounter with Richard replays in her mind. She'll kiss Jake's shoulder. He'll rouse and turn to her. They will align in the darkness, her uncovered self against his.

After a few times of this, Jake begins to approach without caution, day or night. He grabs with greed in his hands. She clutches him closer, breathes deliberately close to his ear, watches him tingle. Afterwards, when Jake wears that proud grin, his handsome face gleaming with sweat, Helena refuses to believe she's done anything wrong.

The second time she has sex with Richard they slip away mid-afternoon, taking separate cars and staggering their departures.

She parks blocks away and sneaks down muddy alleys where the gravel strains her ankles and scratches the heels of her shoes, leaving black nicks and nasty brown smudges on the leather. Why she would try to navigate the slushy streets of Welltown in a partial thaw after the prevailing westerly winds melted everything, wearing dress shoes no less, she will never know.

For a scarf, she wears the multi-layered weave of rust and brown in cowgirl style, tied at the back, swooped over her breasts, the playful triangle marked by miniature pom-poms along the edges. Oh my, yes. Later, she will look back and cringe. What did she think she was doing?

After sneaking up the stairway solo because they decided it was safer, she stands in front of Richard's apartment, watching the elevator, prepared to rush down the hall if it stops on his floor. Although he doesn't answer the knock, the doorknob turns in her hand. Safely inside, she kicks off her tattered shoes and walks through the unlit apartment to the open bedroom door. Her feet sink into the bedding he tossed onto the floor before she arrived. He's waiting on the open sheet, his flesh warming the dimmed room, pink skin on a hairless chest. She peels off her clothes.

In a tight embrace with a body she does not know well, she forgets all the years she did not feel. Sex with her husband is better than ever. What she's doing is not only for herself. Except skin has its own kind of memory, and its thoughts of Jake that overtake her mind in the peak of the moment. How she likes the roughness of his touch when he's trying to be gentle. How his wide chest pressed near hardens her nipples. In contrast, Richard is so thin she feels like she's hugging herself.

When she opens her eyes, Richard is watching. His pale face is vulnerable. Without the ponytail, his hair seems thinner. A mouse-like whimper leaves his mouth. Too late, Helena wishes she'd looked away. She sees herself as if from a distance, cannot believe what she has done, wishes she were somewhere else, is eager to be gone.

Richard pats her thigh. She rolls away and looks at her wristwatch. "We're late," she says, getting out of bed. Even before they left the office, she knew they'd be rushed to make it back on time for the faculty meeting.

She's into her bra and panties before he leaves the bed. He only gets up after she's started fixing her face. Leaning towards his dresser mirror, she begins to spread the coral glow over her lips. She's not now wearing her putty angora sweater with the swoop neck. From where it rests on the table, her thick weave of a scarf offers no help. She's not at home, he's not her husband, and it's more than cleavage now. On the shiny surface of the mirror, her gaze creeps upward from her breasts to her neck, where the skin sags and folds. She lifts her chin and the results are worse. Her skin is a tent and she's tightened the cords.

She's only covered half her upper lip when he turns the ceiling light on.

"There you go. Isn't that better? You can see yourself now."

One thing about Jake, he came forward of his own accord and admitted his mistake. Until she'd escaped Richard's bedroom, rushed back to work, and arrived at the faculty meeting with messed up hair and the smell of a man who is not her husband, she hadn't realized how brave Jake had been. She understands now what he meant all those years earlier when he said he hated himself.

As soon as she gets home from work, she throws her idiotic scarf into the garbage and tucks the angora sweater into the back of her closet. The sweater was stupidly expensive, and she hopes one day she may no longer hate it. She scrubs herself in the shower, lingering under the hot spray, watching the soap scum wash down the drain.

A little while later, Jake gets home and finds her lying on the couch with a fleece blanket on top of her. She's spread out in front of the TV, watching a talk show. He perches on the edge of the sofa. His salt-and-pepper hair only makes him more handsome. "What's up? You sick?"

She mutes the volume and drags herself into a sitting position. The fleece falls from her lap. "No. I'm fine. Got home early and thought I'd relax."

He joins her on the sofa. She feels the warmth of him at her side. He kisses her hair and she turns to him. Their lips join. He tastes like coffee and the orange he has every afternoon. Her hand reaches for his cheek, rests there gently, aching to touch what may soon be lost. She's no longer confused about whose flesh she's touching.

"Is something wrong?" he asks.

"No, no. I'm tired, that's all."

There was a time she would never have lied to her husband.

They'd shared all their secrets until the morning he'd confessed what he'd done. She was used to seeing him with reddened cheeks and heavy eyelids. He came home looking ruined after most shifts. But the way his mouth sagged, the way his fearful eyes latched onto hers, she'd known it was more than exhaustion. After he'd told her, she'd held a pillow to her chest. She'd sent him away. He'd left without argument. Then he'd waited patiently, was waiting still, for her to forgive him.

Faithfully by her side on the sofa, he does not seem concerned by the silence. His attention is drawn to the TV. She turns up the volume and tries not to change the rhythm of her breathing. She should tell him something straightforward, like I had sex with a person from work. It didn't mean anything. And I wish it never happened.

A week later, Richard calls her into his office. Lately, their communications have all been at the reception counter where she works within easy watch of the wide hallway. She finds the passing by of learners at the turning of the hour comforting.

This is the first time since they last slipped away to have sex that he's asked to see her alone. She sits primly with her skirt tucked around clenched thighs. A fresh pad of paper rests next to the pen in her hand. The proposal is due in less than a week and they need to focus.

Even when he rises from his desk, she avoids his face. A dean gets a large office, at least by academic standards. There is plenty of room for pacing around, a whiteboard on which to explore ideas, and file cabinets that lock. The paint on the spot of the wall where the photo of his wife used to hang is cleaner than everywhere else. He's never chosen to put up something else in its place. All those hours in his office, and she never noticed before.

He walks behind her. She hears the door click. Moments later, he's back at his desk. He reaches across the surface cluttered with coiled reports and file folders and notepads. The fluorescent lights overhead give off a faint hiss as his fingertips graze the back of her hand. Colleagues are talking in the office next door. If a person listens closely enough, they can hear what they're saying.

She slips out from under his fingers, backs out of her chair, goes to the door and re-opens it. Then she reports back to his desk, standing at attention awaiting instruction, unsure how to proceed.

Richard sighs, removes his glasses, washes his face with open palms, then looks at her with such disappointment she almost wants to apologize. Without the shaping lines of his glasses, his eyes look old and tired, small within pockets of weary skin, crow's feet at their corners.

"What's wrong?" he asks.

"I can't do this anymore."

After Jake told her he'd been unfaithful, Helena slept with her back raised against him. She wouldn't acknowledge his touch or attempts at conversation. She'd hand the kids over to him when it was time for their baths. She'd allow him to kiss each of their children goodnight before she tucked them in.

Then one day, Jake came home late, soaked in the yeasty

smell of beer. The alcohol made him brave. She was leaning back in her favourite overstuffed chair, watching TV, when he dropped to his knees in front of her and reached for her limp hand.

"You have to talk to me," he said. "We need to settle things."

She yanked herself free, gave him a glare. Then, ever so slowly, she raised the remote control, pointed it at the TV, and pressed the power button. "Fine, then talk."

"You need to decide. Take me back and love me, or throw me out because we can't keep living this way. I'm sorry for what I did. Believe me, I hate myself. But it won't ever happen again." He collapsed forward. His face dropped from view. All she could see was the round of his shoulders and his brush-cut head.

The back of her knees hugged the edge of the chair. She looked beyond him at the contents of their living room. Toasted Os in a red plastic bowl, scattered pieces from a wooden puzzle, a single unpaired pink baby sock. She thought of some other life with some other man, one who is not a firefighter, one who was safe from the eager gaze of other women.

"Okay, okay. I'll try." She'd grabbed his arm and tugged him upwards.

A few days after she tells Richard it is over, Helena is in bed with her husband. Underneath a down duvet, they claim separate spots on the supportive surface. They could reach out and touch if they wanted. Stacks of pillows cushion their backs. This is their nightly ritual.

They have been reading for almost an hour when Jake sets

his book on the night table and rolls onto his side. He strokes her arm, his rough fingers turning every tiny hair on end. Utterly still, she cherishes the slow, even strokes over her bare skin. Each time his fingers rise to the air, she knows they will return.

Laying down her book, she turns toward him. She buries her face in his chest, hoping he doesn't want to talk and can be satisfied with her body close to his. She does not feel his warmth, too many systems in shutdown to prevent catastrophic failure. The whole time she's had a book propped on her lap, turning pages at regular intervals, she hasn't really been reading. Her brain desperately tries to piece together meaning. Is there a plan that does not involve complete annihilation? He has a right to know what she's done and be given the choice of whether he wants to forgive her.

"Let me look at you," he says, pushing her away, holding her at arm's length.

No longer propped up with pillows, he does not block the glare from his bedside lamp. It makes her eyes water. She squints.

"You've been quiet lately. Is something wrong?"

"It's my job," she says. "I don't like it anymore. It's not what I thought it would be. I think I'll find something different."

Jake never learns why their life switches direction. Maybe he assumes he's finally been forgiven. He stops trying so hard, lets her pick up her own shoes. She gives him foot rubs, leaves him in peace to watch hockey, takes her own car to be washed.

If only she can remain strong, Jake will never have to suffer.

She devotes herself to making him feel loved, small things, like their new nightly ritual. "Time for bed," she'll announce before hitting the stairs. He'll follow close behind. Any faster and they'd be running. Her feet barely land on the carpeted stairs. His hot breath reaches out, worms down the back of her neck, makes her hurl her body forward.

They undress on opposite sides of the room. He unbuttons his trousers, opens his zipper. She gradually unwinds her black silk scarf, turns down her eyes, afraid to be vulnerable but yielding to that urgent need to be touched.

They meet on their bed, where they have held their marriage for decades. They embrace on cool beige sheets, the bedding tossed aside. Her nipples feel nothing under the cushioning bra she refuses to remove. Jake's face is blank. He does not whimper. He never realizes his wife is watching or that sometimes she touches lightly on a body memory of another man, not because she misses him, but to find again her uncovered self, to bring their relationship back into balance.

After the sex, they rest with legs intertwined. She turns her cheek to his chest. Her drooping eyes barely focus, yet she catches the silver glistening. She'd never noticed before the salt and pepper matching the hair on his head. Her eyes travel the length of his torso, linger at his groin, confirm her suspicions. Ever changing with the light, all she has to do is shift the angle of her head and the hairs turn dark. For a moment, it doesn't seem possible, but she rolls her head back to the resting position, and the glint of silver returns.

Your Body Was Made for This

Brianne joined the outside world puffy-eyed with a surly brow and a flattened nose. Her crinkly mouth yowled, and her blueish fingers clutched the air like claws. Bowed legs dangled from her distended torso. Her oversized head sunk into rounded shoulders. She was neckless.

Everything was out of proportion, not the least of which her potential. She contained two million eggs, her lifetime quota, or so the world believed at the time. Later, the notion that females couldn't generate new eggs proved false, but by then, the damage had been done. Brianne and other girls like her learned their most essential purpose was to guard an ever-dwindling stash and hope one day a smooth, pure egg hatches into a new neckless creature yowling at the open air.

"It's a girl," said the doctor.

Sloppy with anaesthetic, Brianne's mother smiled. The faint red coffee cup-sized stain on her baby girl's cheek would soon disappear. In those days, most babies needed to be tugged into the world, as her mom well knew. She'd delivered twice before.

· 2 ·

Brianne has baby dolls with luscious cheeks. She tucks them under a blanket in a miniature carriage and feeds them with a milk bottle that magically drains without ever losing a drop. She's practising for later, getting ready to be a grown-up mom. The dolls wear pink bonnets with elastic chinstraps and white leather shoes that fit over their stiff plastic feet. Watch out for those feet. They're likely to get punched in, twisted or cracked should the doll grow too adventurous for her own good.

From the minute she's able to keep herself upright, Brianne never stops twirling and skipping and hiding from adults. Her braids are forever coming undone, and the pink barrettes meant to hold them in place are always getting lost under the pine needles below the row of trees in her backyard. She climbs whatever tree she chooses faster than her mother cares to notice. Where the branches have been trimmed, she knee-pinches her way up the trunk. She comes to rest under the cover of sticky boughs with needles that poke her if she's not careful.

"Brianne, you crazy girl. Where are you now?" Her mother's hands are on her hips, the elbows pointed outwards, sharp as arrows. Above the cat's-eye glasses that twinkle in the sunlight, her mother's pencilled-in eyebrows pinch.

If only she'd think to glance upward, she'd catch Brianne.

Instead, she walks away, and Brianne grows bored of hiding. It isn't any fun without somebody looking for you.

She slides down coarse bark, getting pinesap on her yellow dress with puff sleeves. Sneaking across the velvet lawn, she creeps in through the back screen door and tiptoes up the steps from the landing. But she never makes it past the kitchen. Her mother snatches her by the ear with long red fingernails and drags her to the washroom, where she scrapes off the pinesap with a nail brush.

And afterwards, in the bedroom with the princess lace curtains, her mother fixes Brianne's fly-away hair, changes her dress, and sits her down in the corner where the dolls in the baby carriage have been waiting.

Her mother places the dripless bottle into Brianne's hand. "What kind of mother are you? Look at your girls. They're starving."

· 3 ·

By the time she starts school, Brianne has plenty of spine for the white cotton turtleneck she wears under an orange jumper with fat buttons down the front. A matching orange band holds back the shiny black hair her mother gives one hundred brush strokes every night. The girl must have gotten that hair from her father, thinks her platinum-blond mother.

The Welltown Public School System has its standards, and girls are not permitted to wear pants. Every morning, Brianne yanks on her cotton panties and tugs up the leotards she's forced to wear winter and summer. There are two colours to choose from: black and white. Not that it matters. Whichever pair she's wearing, the crotch is forever sagging. The egg-white folds of skin where her legs meet sweat, stick and rash. She's constantly scolded by teachers for squirming in class, and she can never say why.

A week into grade 1, Brianne already knows life is unfair. She's tried on her brother's pants.

· 4 ·

In grade 5, all the girls are herded into the school gym for a top-secret assembly. With the knees of their leotard legs pressed together, they sit on fold-out metal chairs arranged in a tight semicircle. The lights go off, and a young woman fills the projector screen with a face pure as milk and auburn hair flowing over a peach sweater that shows the curves of emerging breasts. Her image grows smaller and moves to the side. Text flashes onto the screen, "Congratulations, you're becoming a woman."

Each girl receives a brochure and a maxi-pad in a pretty plastic wrapper of white lace over powder blue. The brochure features the same beautiful girl, sitting pensively in her bedroom one minute, cycling through a city park the next. Having your period should no longer be thought of as a curse. That's what the brochure says.

For months after the assembly, all the girls whisper, "Do you have your period yet?" Brianne is the first, not that she tells anyone. The place where her legs meet does more than rash now. She's not allowed to call it blood, so the brochure says. It feels like diarrhea.

Now she's reached puberty, Brianne has half a million eggs. All the others, one and a half million bubbles of infinite potential—gone without her ever noticing.

· 5 ·

Cramping, bloating, sore and swollen breasts, headaches, mood changes and irritability, not to mention depression. These are only a few of the monthly symptoms. By junior high, it's a standing joke amongst the girls. Watch out for so and so. She's on the rag.

Now that Brianne is in regular need of feminine products, her mother swells with possibilities. She pictures a granddaughter in a blush-pink, burn-out-lace dress with a rose on the shoulder and a grandson in a smart blue vest with a grey tie and white shirt. She'll take one grandchild in each hand as she enters the cathedral for Sunday Mass.

Crow's feet cause her concealer to crack. Dull grey invades her used-to-be head of golden hair. Because of the crinkles that ruin her upper lip, fire engine red is no longer a viable option. The only hope Brianne's mother has is for the future.

She plunks a jumbo box of tampons onto Brianne's dresser. "When you're older, you'll become a mother." She pats her daughter's belly. "Even though that's a long time from now, your body's getting ready." And there it is, predestined by biology, Brianne's future has been planned.

· 6 ·

Brianne finds herself a hammer under the boxes of drywall screws and doorknob hardware in her father's neglected workshop. She likes the weight of its head, the power in the handle. In the backyard, under cover of pine trees, she practises swinging until she can drive a nail into the fence with three sharp strokes.

By grade 11, everyone's deciding what they're going to be. While other girls go into nursing and teaching, Brianne wangles a job helping a farmer build his barn. An aging Ukrainian without sons, the farmer doesn't care she's a girl. He's seen her wield a hammer. She stays the entire summer. His wife feeds them cabbage rolls, sauerkraut and pierogies. Brianne sleeps under a homemade quilt in their guest room with the slanted ceiling.

In the fall, she returns to the city and fights her way into the carpenter apprenticeship program, the first girl ever accepted. During the boom, when there aren't enough workers, she gets on with a crew building high-rises. Brianne likes climbing ladders. The drag of a tool belt on her hips gives her swagger. She wears baggy t-shirts over thick canvas coveralls and cuts her hair extra short.

Her mother serves her tuna casserole and says, "Men don't like butch girls."

· 7 ·

Every month an ovary releases a ripened egg. If an eager sperm happens to be swimming nearby, it gloms onto the egg, and without further need of ceremony, the two become one. The fertilized egg nestles into the warmth of the womb. There, the fetus lives for ten months, growing and waiting to be born.

This is how it's always been for all women everywhere. Not so for Brianne. She's born into a new era. Every night at bedtime, she pops a tiny pill from one of the twenty-one chambers in the plastic disk that comes in its own compact, like makeup powder.

Not only does the magical combination of hormones stop ovulation, it thickens the mucus sent out by the cervix. Think of it as a force field right inside her. Sperm cannot get through. Plus, under the influence of the pill, her womb doesn't welcome nesting. Even if a sperm breaks through the force field, the egg will not prosper. Threefold protection.

It's less about "doing it" than about avoiding the consequences should "it" happen. Brianne knows better than to tell her mother. She visits a downtown clinic. The doctor is a young woman herself. No questions asked.

· 8 ·

Arms brushing, eyes searching, fingers squeezing, palms pressing hard. Although it happens on the work site where she's an apprentice, it's worse during in-school training. Tough guys corner her at the tool board, come up behind when she's working the band saw. Butch girls get special treatment. Her mother doesn't know.

Brianne thinks Neil is different. The way he stammers his suggestion that maybe they could catch a movie, go for pizza. The way his eyes stick to the dirty linoleum on the lunchroom floor. The way he fumbles the plastic wrapping on his ham and cheese. She thinks he's gentle.

The movie is at a drive-in. Neil takes her there in his rusted-out brown station wagon. During intermission, he coaxes her into the cargo area in the back. They lie together on sleeping bags that smell of mildew. At first, she enjoys cuddling, the wiry arms of a boy squeezing her middle, the crush of his kisses.

Then, Neil forgets to ask permission. He yanks off her jeans and panties, loses himself. Pegged down by a single moment of indecision, she's caught unprepared on her back. She should've knee-pinched herself up a tree.

But he folds her arms to her sides and pins her between his bulging thighs. Before she can say no, he seals her lips with his. A hot knife burns at the spot where she pees, stabs deep and cuts her open. Afterwards, real blood mixes with his release. He offers her a tissue.

· 9 ·

Brianne no longer trusts the pill. It doesn't provide the right kind of protection, plus she sees no reason to continue withholding eggs. Let those bubbles of infinite potential drop where they may. She can't spend them fast enough. With nothing that might glom on and no reason for ceremony, the living pearls pass right through her.

When it comes to force fields, she'd rather have one closer to her face. She signs up for women-only karate. Filling more space than her five-foot frame might imply, Sensei Nohara leads the small group through basic techniques, her raven braid swaying and snapping, her dark eyes fierce. The five women in the class have only one thing in common. The youngest is model thin, and the oldest has wobbly skin. Together, they learn shizentai, the centring pose. Each lays claim to personal space, each stakes out the spot from which they will fight, the spot from which they will not be moved.

Brianne inhales, softens her knees and finds the ground. She straightens her neck. Her shoulders move up, rotate back and lower down. A fullness comes into her spine, begins at her groin and rises into the air above her head. She will never be pinned down by indecision again. With a steady exhale, her feet shift into a parallel stance. She will not be moved.

· 10 ·

For years, the force field stops all comers-on. Then Dylan appears, and the force field has no effect on him. Actually, he likes it. They meet in Chiang Mai, Thailand, where they're both volunteering to rebuild a school damaged by a flood. She notices him on the plane ride over, sees him walking the tarmac in steel-toed boots dirtier than hers.

Later, they knock shoulders at the luggage carousel. Their backpacks are identical right down to the royal blue colour. The only difference is the West Coast Trail badge Brianne sewed onto hers a few years earlier after she ran the entire trail before the sun set on a single day.

When she spots the tip of her backpack on the carousel, she doesn't realize his is riding piggyback. They dive for their luggage at the same moment. Brianne bumps him hard. His hip slams the ridge of the carousel, and she tilts sideways in the opposite direction. It takes her a couple of steps to regain balance. If he hadn't dropped his pack to the floor and reached for hers, she'd have had to wait until her pack came around the carousel again.

They're officially introduced the next morning at the first meeting of the volunteers. He tilts his hard hat, revealing the red bandana underneath and a face loaded with freckles. With a playful grin, he offers her his gloved hand. "Please don't hurt me," he says.

· 11 ·

On their first date, they go rock climbing at Crazy Horse Buttress. At first cautious with being entrusted to each other, within five minutes of climbing they both know they're safe. Pure, delicious focus, the rhythm of movement, all of it shared. The Dangerous Joy route was one of the first to be bolted. The holds are huge, although not always easy to find. When she watches Dylan climb around the overhang, each of his moves certain and careful, his courage matched by humility and accentuated by grace, she knows he's the one. She follows his lead, and soon they're both on the spacious ledge, stunned by the wide view of lush peaks under a soft grey sky. They shake out their arms, lean in, and kiss.

They wait for sunset back in Chiang Mai, tasting life on the crowded street where green beans and carrot slices jiggle in a gargantuan wok and pork skewered on bamboo wisps tangy smoke. Their hands interlace as they meander past overloaded displays of brightly coloured paper lamps and silk parasols.

In front of a temple, open-mouthed dragons stretch down

the steps. A golden Buddha sits at the back of the hall, above shelves that hold lush towers of pink and white and yellow blossoms. When Dylan leads her back to his room, she never considers denying either of them.

Years later, they are still embraced, faithful without marriage. They have a simple understanding, a shared experience that does not need to be registered or signed. It does not require a blood test.

Dylan is first to say it: "Not that I don't love children. I just don't see myself becoming a parent."

· 12 ·

Brianne's sister delivers on the promise of a grandson in a smart blue vest. When the boy is born, Brianne and Dylan are in Slovakia. They don't meet their nephew until he's four months old.

But they're home for the arrival of the niece who will one day wear a blush-pink dress with a rose on the shoulder. At the hospital, mere hours after the birth, Val places the swaddled hope with a puckered face into Brianne's unsteady arms. "Here you go. You hold her."

Brianne can't say *no thank you*, or *not at the moment please*, *maybe later*, or *let's wait and see*. All she can think is *better not drop her*. And *how long before I can give this fragile creature back?*

Val rocks in her chair. Her eyes move from Brianne's face to the babe cradled in her arms. "Relax. She likes you. Your body was made for this."

Those perfect nails on tiny fingers, the skin so translucent a person can see the veins underneath. Brianne touches the miniature hand, and it grabs hold of her big calloused finger.

Her sister smiles. "One day soon, you'll have a baby of your own, Brianne. A tiny creature will look to you for food, shelter, comfort, safety. That's when you'll learn the true meaning of love. It's the only way to become about more than yourself."

· 13 ·

A year later, Brianne notices her breasts getting sore. For several days, she releases herself from her bra the minute she gets home. One night, Dylan tries to draw her into a hug, and she yowls. She steps back. His arms hang uselessly. Empty space lingers between them, but their eyes remain connected.

She finds a lump the size of a poker chip on her left breast. Months later, neither of them has fully adjusted to what's happening, but she makes a brave choice, her bravest yet. She offers both breasts, although she does not have to. They could wait and see. But she would rather smooth Dylan's forehead now, take the panic from his hazel eyes and continue their climb. She refuses to wear a lone bag of flesh, sagging and aging beside a reconstruction or a scar. It is her choice, and she would rather be wiped clean.

After the chemo, they give her an injection for her white blood cells that makes her bones ache. Dylan brings her ginger tea and soda crackers. They sit in silence.

On the fourth chemo treatment, a clump of black hair comes off in her hairbrush. When the volunteers arrive, Dylan insists on shaving his head first. Afterwards, they press their naked heads together, both of them afraid. All thoughts of self have been scraped away. Their unadorned skulls have room only for each other.

· 14 ·

A year and a half later, the doctors pronounce Brianne NED: no evidence of disease. Maybe she and Dylan will live out their days together, continue to travel, she will see his wrinkled freckles, they will laugh. But can she be sure he will never be left alone? There is one way she could be certain.

Brianne tells Dylan she'd like a baby. He frowns. "After you're recovered," he says. "We'll talk about it then."

Even at menopause, ten thousand eggs remain. All that potential unable to ripen in withering ovaries. Shortly after she's labelled NED, Brianne stops menstruating at forty-five. This is something that can happen to women in mid-life who undergo chemo, the doctors tell her.

· 15 ·

People say cancer is a teacher. Brianne thinks only a person who hasn't gone to school would say a thing like that, but she did deepen a conviction she's held close since she was an innocent young woman in the cargo area of a rusted-out brown station wagon. Don't grieve too hard over what you've lost, or you risk missing what you have.

On a warm summer afternoon, while on a hike in an alpine valley a few hours from Welltown, jagged peaks layered in rust and grey rise behind a turquoise lake. Dylan and Brianne run screaming, fingers interlocked, into a glacial lake. They have nothing on but water shoes. Others might consider this reckless behaviour for people in their seventies.

Afterwards, they dry off under the sun on cushy moss beside the lake. She runs her fingers through his grey hair. He kisses the scars on her chest. She brings her body to his and his to life. They meet skin to skin, and unafraid, in the open air.

The Point of
Failure

I awoke to the sickly sweet aftertaste of sugar. A mushy glob
of half-chewed frosted cereal was still in my mouth from the
night before. What kind of idiot goes to sleep without swallowing their food?

I peeled back sticky eyelids, and there he was. Jayden, larger
than life, fully dressed and cleanly shaven. He was shaking his
head with a hand over his mouth like any second he might
ralph.

"Oh my God, what is that?" His eyes widened. "Go to the
bathroom and spit that out. . . . You disgust me."

I forced the chunky wad down, swallowing hard. But I could
not get rid of the taste.

"For once, Grace, stop pretending. You don't want to
change."

I hauled my sweaty back up against the cold wall, and he

turned away, no longer caring to look at me. His jacket waited at the foot of our bed, his suitcase next to our door.

He stood at the bedroom window, peering outside. "I can't believe I ever thought we could be happy. You've ruined everything."

A year earlier, we were the poster couple of weight loss. Between us, we'd dropped 180 pounds. We were featured on the Slimmer You website, me in a flirty white dress, him in sexy black jeans. With my fair skin and blond hair, people said I looked like Marilyn Munroe. Jayden could not keep his hands off me. He was constantly eyeing me up and saying he liked it hot.

He plastered my image all over the internet. Strangers looked me up and down. Good mother, why could they not leave me the hell alone? Everyone took my measure, laying bets for how long it might last. Well, yeah. . . . Six months later, I weighed more than ever. Marilyn's ugly twin, bloated beyond recognition, fit only for the cover of a tabloid.

Bracing myself with both arms, I hoisted my legs over the edge of the bed. My weight sunk into the floor, a familiar cramp tugging my heels, but I managed to haul myself to the window.

"Please, Jayden. I'll try harder." I reached for his shoulder and his arms lashed out, knocking me off balance, sending me backwards. My rump banged against the bedpost, the blow causing an instant deep ache, and then I landed on the floor.

"I'm sorry," he said, crouching near. With one hand gripping my forearm and the other bracing my back, he helped me onto my feet. Fool that I am, for a moment, I thought maybe there was a chance for us.

But he backed away slowly, collecting his coat and his suitcase. "There's nothing more I can do for you," he said, turning away.

In elementary school, they called me Cream Puff. In junior high, Fat Ass. While other girls were proud to fill their first bra, for me puberty was a new reason to hate myself. If only I'd remained flat-chested, boys might've left me alone, but my breasts were large and floppy and spilled out of the top of my t-shirts.

I begged Mom to buy me hoodies so I might cover myself. She said she couldn't find my size, which was what she said most times when I asked for clothes. She thought I didn't know it embarrassed her to go shopping with me.

I walked the school hallways alone. No girl would be caught dead with the likes of me. Cool guys, however, now they had interest. I could not get rid of those boys, hounding me every chance they got, panting behind me, growling. They'd bite my butt with mean fingers, clamping down until they'd left bruises. They'd punch my breasts with hardened fists, wiping their knuckles on their jeans afterwards.

No matter how fast I walked, there was no escaping. One day, the top dog, this guy named Lyle, with greasy red hair and acne, pinned me against the lockers. He smelled like a wet ashtray and man scent. You know, that musky, beasty odour extra ripe on adolescent boys.

I stood there as he held a pen to my face, cowering, my fat thighs trembling.

"Bet you'd bleed gravy," he sneered.

Mom did her best to teach her girl restraint, preloading my dinner plate, refusing to buy chips or chocolate of any kind, trying to convince me fat-free, sugarless ice cream was a treat. She had no idea how resourceful I could be.

I'd steal money from her purse, bags of cookies from grandma, and handfuls of those cheap red-and-white peppermints people had in glass bowls on their coffee tables. On the afternoons I gave in and gorged myself after school, I'd fold the wrappings small and throw them into the tampon receptacle in the grocery store washroom.

All through high school, I knew I would never make the grade. School dances, the grad ceremony, friends to sign my yearbook—all that was for girls small enough for ready-to-wear sizes, girls who didn't have fat breasts, who weren't a lard butt.

When I was accepted into the computer sciences program at a western university on full scholarship, I was glad to leave. Sharing a dorm room made it hard to keep secrets, and residence food was nasty. I dropped thirty pounds without trying in the first month.

But I never shed down to the glamour girl trapped inside. She'd raise her head out of the gooey hole now and then. I'd catch sight of her flirty smile when no one was watching. If I sucked in my cheeks, I saw her elegant face, its strong lines and angles. If I curled my shoulders over my chest, I knew her true width.

That year, I tried everything: cleanses, avoiding bad carbs, avoiding fat, taking magic supplements, fasting, sniffing peppermint, hypnosis. Each new strategy cost me more hope. There were vending machines on every floor of every building on campus, and my pockets jangled with spare change. A stash was unnecessary when there were quiet washroom cubicles.

When I graduated computer sciences with distinction, I left weight loss behind me. I started pinning back my hair in a severe bun and wearing a pocket protector in my shirts.

My first job at the college was as a junior instructor. I'd put in time, like every other sap, at a high-tech sweatshop, the only female on the coding team. Five years of that, head down and grinding it out, only to have some skinny boy in a suit take claim for my work.

Students laughed their heads off at me waddling around the front of the classroom, stepping in the trash can and kicking it across the floor. I never minded, so long as it kept their attention. My student evaluations were better than anyone's. The other instructors hated me, how I was so confident in spite of my size, the way I kept pace with technology, how I seemed to dream in code. Eventually, I taught their asses and became dean.

It was well after Jayden had put me on a diet that I decided to start exercising. They gave staff free access to the fitness centre, so there was that. But, honestly, I think I tried it because

Jayden had nothing to do with it. My idea, my butt. I started easy, spinning four days a week on a bike going nowhere. I kept my head down in the exercise room, plugged into Motown. You know, Jackson Five and Stevie Wonder. I'd get so into the music I'd forget I was not alone.

But in the locker room, I'd have to unplug and listen to the gathering of lost souls. From twenty-somethings to fifty-year-olds, women shared the same obsessions. They viewed themselves as renovation projects that had run off schedule and over budget.

I'd catch them at the full-length mirror, sizing themselves up. *Just ten more pounds, that's all I need to get rid of. . . . Once it settles in, back fat's impossible to remove. . . . I must be losing weight in my fingers. My gut's the same size it's always been.*

Those women had no idea what it was like to have real problems with your weight. It made me want to puke, but I'd gulp it down and keep moving. I worked out in the early morning because there were fewer people. It'd be dark outside when I signed into the fitness centre, and still, I had to endure those model-thin perfectionists.

There was one woman different from the rest, flat as sheet metal across her chest, muscular everywhere else, and completely, beautifully independent of the whole yahoo circus. Like she lived in her own clean bubble of air, unpolluted by the thoughts that seemed to torture everyone else. She paid no mind to how the other women avoided looking at her.

One day, this wholesome influence was getting dressed next to me. Somehow simply having her near helped the world make more sense. The pocket of air was large enough for two. When she was next to me, I did not feel alone. Someone else bore witness. I was not crazy.

A straight-as-a-stick, frizzy-haired blonde had been standing at that full-length mirror whining about her non-existent hips. They hung the mirror in the small alcove by the door, a final goodbye after a hard workout, a kiss-my-butt reminder of personal failings, as if every woman needed to double-check her appearance before going back into the world.

We'd both seen and heard the entire show, although neither of us encouraged it. That powerhouse of a woman. Oh, she warmed my soul. She waited for Frizz-Head to leave, then she waved the back of her hand and rolled her eyes before giving me a *did you catch that nonsense* look. The two of us burst into giggles, and that's when I knew we'd be friends.

And so, the next day, when she stood in front of my bike, I unplugged the Motown.

"Hi," I said. "My name is Grace."

"I'm Brianne."

I offered her my sweaty hand, and she took it.

"Hey, I've been wondering," she said. "Would you like to team up? I notice we're here same time each morning. . . . The crack of dawn, I like to call it." She had this wicked grin I found so energizing. "It'd be nice to not always work out alone."

To this day, I don't know why she chose me, of all people. "That'd be cool," I said, blubbering a little with the excitement of it.

Nothing like this had ever happened to me before. She had

me under her wing from there on out, no question. I mean, she convinced me to do weightlifting. We found a quiet corner of the exercise room. She started me out on two-pound dumb-bells. Anyone would've thought she didn't see I was fat.

Jayden acted all virtuous after he'd lost weight, but when we first met, he was no different from me. I was in my second year of teaching. He was a salesperson for Hewlett-Packard. Our professional lives brought us into the same room, where our mutual interests soon became clear. At networking lunches, we were the last to push our plates away. I'd see him across the room and notice he was still eating. Later, when most people had stopped and were sipping black coffees, we'd meet at the dessert table, exchanging recommendations at first, then tiny mouthfuls of heaven: his chocolate pecan pie, my lemon black-berry cheesecake.

Our first dates were about finding new foods to share. I gave him a taste for churros; he gave me a taste for lamb chops. He travelled a lot for work. So when he was home, the party broke out. We feasted on it. I mean, really, there was no stopping us when we were together. Neither of us was willing to be the first to admit we were full. Fried chicken and banana cream pie, fries and gravy, milkshakes with whipping cream on top and a maraschino cherry. Call me kinky, but it turned me on the way he'd pinch the cherry between his teeth, making eyes at me. I loved being with him. I'd never been so happy.

After we got married, I gained thirty pounds, and he gained sixty. Neither of us was bothered. We cuddled under lap blan-kets in front of the TV, watching horror movies and romcoms in matching sheepskin slippers, eating popcorn and rocky road ice cream.

If Hewlett-Packard hadn't started giving the high-profile clients to younger salespeople, if Jayden hadn't lost all the hair on top of his head, it might've continued. I remember the night I found him in the bathroom under the bright lights, glaring at himself. I gave him a snuggle from behind, big and fat and warm. At other times, he'd have grabbed my hands and pressed them closer or turned around and wagged his rough hunk of a tongue at me.

Not that night. We'd crossed a line, as I soon learned in the bedroom before lights out. He had a pad of paper and was making a list: 1) Lose weight. 2) Improve my sales record. 3) Show them you're proud to be bald.

The next day, he shaved off all his hair, replacing the black fringe with a gleaming scalp. Soon we had Slimmer You menu plans, calorie-counting apps, and computer-generated bar charts all over the kitchen walls. It wasn't long before I realized he had an extra improvement item on the list, one he'd never written down.

I'd tried to become the person he wanted. I'd almost made it, but I just could not keep up, and I missed the man I'd married. By year's end, he'd lost 120 pounds. That's the size of some women I know. I mean, seriously. I hardly recognized the raw-boned man who emerged. He updated his suits and bought tinted contact lenses to bring out more gold specs in his hazel eyes. His sales record tripled.

It was probably my talent for systems logic that helped me

achieve the little I did. The charts and the formulas, the choice of apps, the number crunching and measurement, the system diagnostics, all of it was powerfully engaging, keeping my mind elsewhere.

Except it wasn't about my mind. It was about my body, and pounds don't lie. The computerized weight scale was configured by Jayden. He had the inside track on such gadgets, what with his job. The robot-head monitor with its nifty blue-tinged screen, the thin bar up the middle, the solid platform firmly on the floor.

Before coffee, before food, we'd say hello to the bathroom scale. He'd go first, his spine lengthening before he stepped onboard. I swear he grew an inch taller at the thought of how good he'd been and the numbers confirmed his virtue.

I'd wait my turn in bare feet on cold marble, surrounded by gleaming clean surfaces, worried about how it might go this time. If I managed to consistently lose weight for a week, he'd buy me a nice blouse. One time I got pearls. But if I gained a single pound, his face would sag, and he'd say, "Do us both a favour, would ya? Tomorrow, just don't bother showing up." Then he'd turn off his beloved weight scale, reaching past me like I wasn't there. "If you refuse to try," he'd add, "that's your business. But don't expect me to watch."

And sure enough, next day I'd do better.

Not long after he'd walked out on me, Jayden returned for more clothes. I stood with my hands in a knot, running scenarios in my head, unable to decide what I should say. He'd heard it all before, and if I'd told him I would lose weight, he would not have believed me.

"Are you making out okay in your new place?" I asked.

"Yeah, it's not bad. Clean, at least, and quiet."

He was staying in a boarding house normally used by students. We'd agreed it was best in the interim while we figured out what to do. I mean, we were still making decisions together, kind of.

He'd loaded his suitcase with silk boxers and merino socks, a couple of the leather suspenders he'd special ordered, his simple black cotton pants and his golf shirts. Ah, yes, the guy had taste.

"Let's leave the finances as they are during our trial separation," he said. He zipped the suitcase, having taken little more than he would for a vacation.

And he'd called it a trial like maybe I still had a chance to prove myself. Since the morning he'd left, I'd been good. The first night on my own, I had a few nuts and a bag of ripple chips with dill dip, but I could not have choked down another mouthful.

That vacant look in his eyes, the way he said there was nothing more he could do for me. If I didn't turn things around, I would lose him. Divorce is the ultimate diet; everyone knows that.

I threw out the chocolate bars, the salted nuts, the expensive licorice allsorts and the jumbo bags of smokehouse barbeque chips. I put myself on a strict diet of one thousand calories a day, filling my gut hole with celery, carrots, and unbuttered popcorn. Throughout the day, I allowed myself small snacks like I'd been told by the online forum I'd started following.

Proper women, not the Slimmer You types, were on that forum, and they shared personal stories about how they'd stopped bingeing. One gal put an elastic band on her wrist. She twanged it whenever she had an unhealthy thought about food. I did the same, and my wrist stung all the time.

Meanwhile, in the exercise room at the crack of dawn, Brianne insisted I build muscle. Before she became a carpentry instructor, she'd worked alongside men on construction sites. While I messed around with dumbbells, she did the real thing, slipping three massive disks on each end of the long bar. She squatted in perfect form and dead lifted with slow, graceful control, her sleek black pageboy cutting across the edge of her jaw.

Years before we met, Brianne had a radical mastectomy on both sides. After the operation, she was unwilling to risk the complications of implants and she hated padded bras. The one time I dared ask, she told me plain and simple, "I'm too old to wear falsies."

She coached me through the process, telling me over and over again that I needed to push hard right to the point of breaking. Weeks and weeks passed before I improved. Muscle comes from the repair of microscopic tears. It's necessary to sustain damage but not too much damage. I understood damage, although I was not so familiar with the magical process of repair.

Then it happened. It freaking bloody well happened! I think it was her watching, that look of confidence. She had an inner power and she lent me some. I'd already done ten bicep curls and did not feel exhausted. There was still more in the muscle, and I kept going.

"Excellent, Grace. Well done. You can do it." Jayden would never have believed it, but Brianne was not surprised. Nodding, she watched me squeeze another curl from my flabby arm.

"*Eee. Yowww*," I said, elegant as ever. "This is getting hard."

"Keep your form. Good," she reminded me as I slowly did another rep. She'd set aside her own training to support mine. She was that kind of friend.

On the third rep, partway through, I knew I could not do more. It took all my concentration, all my courage, to finish that single one, the realest one.

"Way to go. You're amazing. You did it!"

When Jayden asked to meet for lunch, we'd been living apart for six months, and I was thinking maybe it was permanent. But he said he wanted to talk about the relationship. And I thought maybe I'd get a chance, maybe if he saw what I'd done, maybe we could be together again.

I waited for him in the cafeteria run by the culinary arts students. They served up delicious food daily, as everyone who worked at the college knew. I was holding a place in line for him when he stepped towards me, power walking as usual, in his casual black suit jacket and jeans, his scalp gleaming.

After all the effort I'd put into imagining his reaction, for the longest time he failed to notice. He was too busy watering his mouth with all that food. When the well-loaded plate of a stranger sailed by, his eyes were all over the glistening grilled salmon, creamy wild rice, glazed carrots and fragrant squash.

"Want to share a serving?" he said. The familiar look of longing on his face. I could not believe it.

"Ah, sure. That'd be good."

"If we each only have half, there won't be too many calories. And gosh, the salmon looks perfect, doesn't it?"

We were still hunting for a table when I caught him finally sizing me up, from breasts to hips and back to my breasts again.

"You've lost weight," he grinned. "Could be as much as twenty-five pounds. It looks good on you."

I slipped onto a chair and pulled myself to the table's edge. "Thank you," I said, swallowing.

Twisting the cap off his diet pop, he said, "All you have to do now is stick with the plan. Another twenty-five or thirty, and you'll have a waist. You'll be so sexy then."

He loaded his fork with a chunk of salmon and some creamy rice. His cheeks swelled as he chewed. I no longer had any appetite. My salmon sat unattended on my plate, smeared with the sauces from when he'd sliced off my share from his.

And later, I got home from work to find him in our bedroom, hand on the bedpost, waiting. His suitcases were spread open on the bed. Judging from their emptiness, he'd already tucked away his silk boxers, suspenders, and other clothing.

I slumped onto the hard chair we kept in the corner, mostly

as a place to toss dirty clothes. This is what I'd been hoping for, and yet I wish he'd have discussed it with me first.

"You're back, I guess," I said. Six months after he'd bruised my ass. Six months after he'd left me for dead, a fat lump of once-wife still in pyjamas, crying. "Welcome home."

He slid the empty suitcases under our king-sized bed, everything neat and tidy. With the evidence out of sight, he came to me all fatherly and kissed my head. "I can see you're trying, Grace. That's all I've ever wanted."

He guided me down the hall, his arm tucked under my elbow. He'd posted a weight-loss curve with my projected progress on the fridge. "I'm here now. I'll help you."

For supper, we had stir-fry, Jayden's special low-cal recipe. I ate a reasonable portion. The sound of his chewing and swallowing, the smacking of his lips and the glug of water draining down his throat. All of this would've been comforting in the past. He was my eating companion. Swallow for swallow, we'd match each other. Now, I ate alone.

I told myself I'd get used to things. If I wanted to stay married, I'd have to work on it. At least he was here with me. At least he was trying.

We'd always slept facing away from each other; such was our habit. I'd relax my back into the mass of his heat. We stayed in contact, but each with our own air to breathe. He found facing each other claustrophobic.

Things changed after he'd lost weight. Instead of heat, he offered a thin chill that never seemed to warm. That night, while he snored, his body stole all my heat.

And the promise of what lay hidden in the closet under the towels drew me out of bed. My stomach bawled like a big baby, my mouth sucking at nothing. I'd been building a stash for weeks, telling myself it wasn't so bad as long as I didn't eat anything. On random days, I'd grab stuff I wasn't allowed. A chocolate bar from a vending machine, sugar-coated cereal from the grocery store, chips from the gas station.

I ate in the kitchen with my back to the entrance, not watching or listening the way I'd always done. My mouth rooted at the first touch of chocolate. I latched on, sucking fiercely. After a while, all I noticed was blubbery texture, melting fat streaming down my throat, filling my belly, plumping up all that was the visible me, making her bigger and bigger until the pretty girl trapped inside could no longer feel her legs or hear her own heartbeat.

Once the jumbo bar was dissolved inside me, I tossed the silver wrapping into the garbage under the sink. To rid my mouth of the coating, I slugged back ice-cold milk straight from the carton.

Then wiping my mouth, I closed the fridge door and told myself that was all. I could return to the warmth, put baby back to bed. The morning Jayden had walked out on our marriage, he never waited for me to fully wake up. He'd packed before we'd spoken. He didn't care that what he'd said would be the first thing I heard that day. "Go to the bathroom and spit that out. You disgust me." We'd been married for decades, and he had no idea how much he could hurt me.

The milk washed away the food I'd had before and welcomed me to fill myself with more. I stood at the counter, stuffing fistfuls of frosted shredded wheat, the little ones that seem so poppable into my mouth. The dry cereal scratched my gums, stuck in the cracks of my teeth, felt like it crawled up my nose. I gagged and kept stuffing, chewing, swallowing.

The next morning, I awoke yet again with half-chewed food like vomit in my mouth. Jayden stood over me, but I did not give him the privilege. This time I refused to swallow. I spat the sticky glob into the toilet, swept my mouth with a dirty tongue and spat again.

My gut was a dark hole, slushing with rotting food, fermenting with sugar. I may have reclaimed a fraction of dignity, corrected my form when I walked away from him, but there was no denying what happened.

Jayden was waiting outside the bathroom door. He took my hand and led me to the kitchen. He'd already set the empty cereal box and the silver wrapping on the counter. He must have dug them out of the trash.

The wrapping still held the scent of chocolate, and my mouth remembered the thick ooze melting down my throat. My fat thighs trembled underneath my nightgown. I wanted him to hug me.

He shook his head sadly. Like the other time, he was fully dressed and cleanly shaven, although he hadn't yet packed his bags. Perhaps there'd been more he'd been hoping to achieve.

"I don't understand why you do this to yourself," he said, tightening his belt. Although he'd reached his goal weight a long time ago, he was still losing.

"Get out," I said, aching at the thought. "Pack your bags and go." So many microscopic tears, damage that may never repair, and yet I had one more rep in me. I had not failed yet. "You are no help to me. I'm better off on my own."

A confused look crossed his face. We stood like the opponents we'd become, no longer companions, two people at war with each other and themselves. This is how I later saw it. In that moment, I only wanted to die.

For a couple of breaths, nothing happened. Then, *whirr*, *click*, *sizzle*. He was back on. "Fine, but this time it's permanent." He cocked his chin.

Beneath the fake gold sparkle of his ordinary hazel eyes, I caught a hint of something he worked hard to hide. I answered as gently as I could. "Yes, I'm sorry."

The online forum about bingeing said backsliding was common, and if it happened, a person should guide themself gently forward. After Jayden left, I put myself into a chair in front of the dining table. Without appetite, I ate a bowl of cereal and a banana, and I swallowed black coffee.

I organized my workout gear because Brianne would be waiting. She made no comment about my puffy eyes, pale face and lacklustre effort that morning. By the next day, I was ready to try harder. She still had that way of cleaning the air. It didn't matter what others might think, the people who pitied her lack of breasts, the people who thought I was fat beyond redemption.

Soon, there were changes, and they started to spread. I noticed it first in my thighs. They randomly twitched, intense tugs speaking of strength I never knew I had. One morning, after my post-workout shower, I looked down at my naked flesh, past my belly and the most private parts of myself to what was below, and I saw a bulge on the outside of my thigh above my knee.

The morning I did my first dead lift, Brianne waited patiently. She had that way about her, a calming presence. If I'd been unable to complete the lift, we would try again the next day. We took our time setting me up, making sure my body was properly aligned. She fastened a ten-pound disk on each end of the weight bar, and I pointed my toes forward, lifting with the full strength of my hips. Brianne was always talking about the undeveloped power most people carry in that region.

I'd done so well at watching what I ate and exercising I'd started to give myself one small treat a week. After showering and dressing, I headed to the coffee shop on campus for a mochaccino—frothy milk, rich dark chocolate, pungent espresso, and a dollop of real whipping cream.

A long line of students, instructors, and staff shuffled toward the coffee counter. I was next to be served when a group of male students began snickering behind me. I was not unused to students laughing at me, as I explained earlier. But standing in line for coffee, I figured they must be laughing at each other. Casually, I turned around to see if I might get in on the joke. They turned silent, which by itself was not such a big thing, except for the smirks, those smug *I know something you don't* smirks.

The barista leaned across the counter. She lowered her voice.

"I think maybe your shirt has come untucked," she said. "You might want to pull it down."

The students could not hold it a minute longer. They started to howl.

And that's when I saw it, the two-inch gap above the waist of my pants, the muffin-top roll of pale flesh bulging there. When I'd purchased the black acrylic shirt, the sales clerk told me the gathered fabric along the sides made me look thinner.

Because I'm fat, does that make me public property? I got it all the time, not only from Jayden. *You have such a pretty face*, relatives said. *But you'd look better if you were more healthy*. And even after I'd successfully lost weight, when I ought to have been praised, I got the sideways glance and the low-voiced question my skinny co-worker could not keep to herself. *Now you're normal-sized, you won't ever let yourself weigh that much again, will you?*

I'd been hoping for better. Ever since the day I saw my thigh muscle, I'd been sneaking glances. Honestly, I liked the curve of muscle above my knee. I told myself in a few months, I'd trace the line all the way from my foot to my hips. I'd allow myself to see every inch of what I'd become. And when I did, I might be surprised. I might not hate myself.

Then those boys in the coffee shop showed me for what I was—a woman too stupid to know she was fat. I fled the coffee shop and the boys who would hound me. I threw my mochaccino in the garbage and took refuge in the nearest washroom. Once inside a cubicle, I yanked down my pants. And what did I see? Belly flesh hanging in chicken skin folds over my pubic area. Stretch marks, although I'd never been pregnant.

Back in my office, I pretended I could be strong. Within an hour, I was at the concession, buying the largest chocolate bar they sold and salt and vinegar potato chips. I settled into a bathroom stall in another part of campus, making sure the door was bolted. I crammed the junk into my mouth, swallowing without chewing like I was trying to choke myself. Afterwards, I stuffed the wrappers in the tampon garbage.

It took Brianne weeks to convince me to return to the gym. I only did it because I didn't want to lose her friendship. She never breathed a word about the weight I'd regained. We went back to the same routine I'd been doing before. Again, I watched her dead lift with slow, graceful control. Again, I marvelled at her confidence and ease. Over time, I made progress, the repair of microscopic tears, over and over again.

The same women who avoided Brianne's face were mesmerized by her undeniable strength. I applauded their humbling. I'd catch them sometimes looking sideways at me, their gaze moving between us.

The day I dead lifted one hundred pounds, I worked perpendicular to the mirror to check my alignment. I lowered the weight bar to the carpet, and Brianne said, "Nice form. Looking good. You can do this."

The walls were solid mirror from floor to ceiling. I usually avoided them. But that day before I stood up, while my muscles were still engaged, I stole a glance, first at my foot and then my calf. A fist of muscle flexed under my skin.

The staff locker room had no change stalls. I was usually

careful to hold my gaze away while Brianne was dressing. That morning, feeling pumped up about the heavy weight I'd lifted, I was not paying attention to where my eyes went. She stepped out of the shower, pulling back the curtain before she'd finished tucking the towel at her chest. I caught the flash of pale skin, and couldn't help staring at the puckered empty spots where there had once been breasts, the pink lines of scars. Ashamed of where my eyes had been, I lowered their lids, hoping she hadn't noticed.

She stood before me, her palms raised as if in praise for each scar. There was no one else in the locker room. She was unafraid and real. "It's okay, Grace," she said. "The breasts are not a vital organ. You can live without them." And she cupped each scar with a warm hand, cuddling herself.

Together, we held this secret as other women came into the locker room, undressing and having a shower, dressing again in the narrow space with an aluminum bench down the centre, the walls crowded with long orange lockers and no change stalls for anyone.

Take Two

· 1 ·

Myrna slid from her mother's womb on a sunny August day in their backyard with a robin cheering from a nearby spruce tree. She landed on warm grass in a gush of body fluids, her mother squatting above. The neighbour, who'd been watering geraniums, saw what happened and rushed over with clean towels and a pot of warm water.

She dropped to the lawn next to Mama and tended the new baby, wiping the thin band of the closed mouth, running a finger from the corner of each sealed eye to the outside of each nostril. A nurse trained in such matters, the neighbour blew on the scrunched-up face and patted the soft back, and when Myrna did not breathe, she placed her mouth over the tiny mushroom-shaped nose and gently sucked.

Next thing they knew, Myrna let loose her very first, "Waah . . . Maaa . . . Ghwaa." Her pale tongue fluttering inside the hollow of her sweet, pure mouth brought Mama to tears.

Ten months earlier, during a blistering snowstorm, under a homemade quilt, Myrna's parents engaged in a naked embrace, and Papa released between twenty and one hundred million sperm. An exact count was not taken, but of the few hundred hoping to fuse with the egg, only one made it in.

· 2 ·

Myrna has her own set of matryoshka dolls. She lines them up on the blue Formica counter. Sometimes, she imagines them as friends, other times family. She has softer dolls with fleshy faces and golden hair, but she loves the bright red, green, and yellow hand-painted dolls Baba gave her best. How each fits within another. How the swaddled baby is loved and protected by all. Mama came out of Baba, she's been told. She herself came out of Mama, and one day a new baby will come out of her.

She stands on the silver-framed chair-and-stool-in-one that they keep in the kitchen. The steps have been folded in. When she gets older, she'll sit on that chair stool. For now, she balances on top of the blue-marble vinyl, leaning over the kitchen counter, watching Mama make pierogies.

If she's good, she gets to help, but never during the dangerous parts when small fingers might get burned. Later, when everything's cooled and Mama's squishing up the tasty mush and adding cottage cheese, that's when Myrna helps.

Bringing the pot to where Myrna leans over the counter, Mama puts the big masher in her little girl's hands. Then, she lifts Myrna up and holds her in place. After all, Myrna's only two, not nearly tall enough to do it alone. Steady over the deep pot, Myrna smashes to her heart's delight.

After the filling is ready, they start the dough. The yolks float briefly in the shallow water of a measuring cup, then Mama whips them with a fork and pours the liquid over the silty mound of flour in a big glass bowl. Pretty soon, everything clumps together. Mama empties the dough onto a floured board to be rolled and squished and rolled some more. The big lump grows smoother, and Mama stops now and then to give Myrna her turn. For Myrna, that's the best part, getting to wiggle her fingers in the pillowy dough, balling the squishy stuff in her fists, rolling the mound over the white dusted board, same as Mama.

· 3 ·

As grade 1 approaches, the situation with Myrna's hair gains urgency. Every night, Mama battles the unruly mass of sandy blond curls that sprout from Myrna's head. Braids come undone, ponytails knot, barrettes fall out. Hiding in the bushes, riding a cardboard box down a grassy slope in a neighbour's yard, stomping in puddles in the cement parking lot at the grocery store—no matter what shenanigans Myrna's been up to, her hair finishes the day a royal tangle.

Before stories and hot milk and lullabies and bed, she must endure detangling. Perched on Mama's lap, Myrna dodges out of the reach of the big wire brush that bites her scalp. It can take over an hour to complete the odious chore. Sometimes, Myrna bleeds.

"Myrna, stop it!" Mama spits in her ear. "Sit still, or we'll be here forever." And later, "Fine, then. Let's chop it off, shall we? Good and short. Snip, snip, snip." Mama uses her fingers as scissors. "We'll make you look just like a boy! How'd you like that?"

The threat's old and dusty. Neither of them believes it. And yet, two months into grade 1, during a particularly fierce battle, out come the gleaming shears with pointy ends. The curls drop dead on the black and white tiled linoleum floor.

Later, when Myrna brushes her teeth and looks in the medicine cabinet mirror, she does not know the person she sees there. And the next day at school, she's the brunt of jokes.

Nobody wants to dance with her during the girl-girl stuff they do in gym. At recess, when she's racing around in a crazy game of tag, she feels a claw grip her shoulder, hears a growl. "Hey, you. What ya think you're doing here? Get yourself over to the proper side of the playground. Right this minute!"

She waits for a reaction from any of the girls in her class, thinking one of them will come to her defence that they won't let her be hauled off like some criminal. But Mr. Fergus is a hulk of a man, and he pushes her to the boy's side of the playground, where she remains alone with shaky legs in her green plaid pants. Only a year earlier, girls weren't allowed to wear pants, not at school, but that's a different story.

· 4 ·

By grade 3, Myrna's well into games only girls play. She carries a smooth black stone in her pocket in case there's an opportunity to hopscotch on the walk home from school. In her own front yard, she draws numbered squares on the short driveway, where she hops through the boxes until Papa drives up and parks their black Beetle.

She can double dutch better than anybody. Mama complains about how quickly she wears down the soles of her Buster Browns. She outlasts all the others, can dance between the ropes the whole day long with people watching and chanting, "Ice cream sundae. Banana split. Myrna's got a boyfriend. Who is it?" She picks some random boy, shouting out the name, and the girls blush at her boldness.

Her truest love is Sally, of the light-filled amber hair, green eyes and giggles. They walk to school together every day. Their houses are on the same block, and their mamas are friends, so they hang out all the time, making tents out of blankets on the grass, licking homemade root beer popsicles, while sitting on the front steps.

For her ninth birthday, Sally has a sleepover. She invites not only her best friend but two other girls. The four of them camp out in Sally's basement on sofa cushions with sleeping bags. They watch Elvis Presley beach movies and stuff themselves with buttery popcorn, extra salted. Then they tuck into their separate cocoons, a flashlight nearby.

Partway through the not-sleeping, Sally comes up with a prank. How about they go outside in bare feet in nothing but nightgowns? They can walk around on damp lawns with the flashlight off and see who gets scared first. They'd have gotten heck if any of their parents knew. Girls aren't safe in the dark. That's why they hold hands.

Sally's palm is hot and sticky, joined with Myrna's. As they stop and look up at the pitch-black, never-ending sky filled with pinprick twinkles, Myrna leans in. She only wants a quick sniff of vanilla. Sally's allowed her to breathe in the creamy yum scent of her shampoo plenty of times, sticking the open bottle under her nose, smiling about it. How's this any different? It seems natural to kiss the amber hair of the person she loves. She'd only meant it as a sign of affection, nothing bad. She never planned it.

But Sally says, "Gross." She pulls her hand free, making an ugly face.

Tina says, "Did you see that?"

Marsha says, "What a weirdo."

The rest of the sleepover is awkward and strange, the other girls clumped together, Myrna off to the side. On Monday, when she goes to pick up Sally for their walk to school, Sally has already left without her.

· 5 ·

A few years later, Myrna no longer cares about tittering girls in nightgowns playing stupid games. Silence is better, a patch of cement in the shadows brings more comfort, and she has books for friends.

Papa grunts, "Do something with yourself, girl. Take your nose out of that book. Go help Mama if you're so bored."

She'd never seen Mama defy Papa before. But her mama turns from the stove with floured cheeks and a sweaty forehead. By this time, Myrna's extravagant hair is styled in a misbehaving pageboy. They keep it out of her eyes with a bright red head-band covered in foam.

"Your head..." Mama says, knocking Myrna's forehead

above the strong lines of her eyebrows. "It's not only for putting a hat on."

But school's got other ideas about a girl's body, and their ideas aren't about what happens in the head. In those days, every female of a certain age is inducted into a private club.

Arranged on wooden chairs in the semi-lit gymnasium with the film ready and loaded, the grade fives wait. A girl-next-door with milky skin, pouty lips and cheeks aglow flashes onto the projector screen set up on a floor stand. Although she's older than anybody watching, the girl's meant to represent them all. "Congratulations, you're becoming a woman," says the text on the screen.

Myrna reads the pamphlet once and tosses it, but the free maxi-pad they give her she leaves on top of the neatly folded undergarments in her drawer. Every time Mama puts away her daughter's freshly washed days-of-the-week panties, she's got to see the pretty plastic wrapper of white lace over powder blue. Yet, she says nothing. Myrna never imagined such an important transition wouldn't be handled by Mama. She's bewildered and terrified at the thought of blood-like tissue coming out of her one day soon and having nobody to talk to about it.

When the day arrives sooner for Myrna than anyone in her class, Mama quietly backs out of the bathroom where they've had their brief whispered exchange and returns with three pads. "I keep them under my bed," she says. "Tell me if you need more."

Sally must hear the clank of the metal box closing or maybe the crinkle of paper when Myrna crumples the strip that covers the sticky line on the pad. Why Sally is listening, Myrna never finds out. But when Myrna leaves the cubicle, her one-time friend is standing guard.

"Really?" sneers Sally, who used to be of the giggles. "You're first!" Her lips twist as she swishes her long mane of glowing hair. Then her bell-bottomed jeans leave the girls' room.

The news does gain Myrna notoriety, at least for a while. Popular girls give her sympathy nods in class, corner her later in the locker room, ask for advice. Boys look at her breasts.

· 6 ·

Sandy-haired Paul has a super hero jawline. He's one of the best-looking boys in high school, even though his voice is breaking. Girls swoon when he walks the halls, fanning their hands and faking seductive eyes at his broad back and tight bottom. Even the coolest seniors, mere months from high-school graduation and normally too proud to talk to young-sters, would do anything for a word from him. Imagine their shock when, of all the girls he could have, he chooses stern-faced Myrna with the untamed hair and the girlish headband. All she's really got going for herself are those globed breasts, a quality other girls have noted in the locker room.

They meet in media club, an oddball group of earnest young people who enjoy hanging out under a red light, developing black-and-white photos of naked trees and empty swings. They'd probably all get into making movies if only they could lay their hands on a Super 8. Paul's the only one so equipped. When Myrna begs to be on his film crew, he respects her enthusiasm.

Soon, the two of them craze with power, stealing his mother's nightgown, rigging up rope to send the white blur rushing down the stairs to his dimly lit basement, firing the rest of the crew when they're five minutes late for a shoot.

The endless hours squabbling over camera angles—it's been a long time since Myrna's had this much fun.

"Let's hang a flashlight inside the gown. The ghost will glow all creepy-like . . ."

"No, shadows are better . . ."

"We could shoot upwards from the floor, Western-movie style . . ."

"Ah, maybe not. Up high from the step ladder? Come on. We have to at least see what it looks like."

After a month of hot and heavy filming, they're ready to edit. They're sitting at his walnut dining table with the cut-glass chandelier dangling above. Their thighs are touching as they find the crap footage from when the camera was jiggly. He's wound forward to the part they want to remove, marked it, and cut the film. He's lined up the two ends and applied the splicing tape, everything is beautifully joined, when all at once he turns to Myrna. His lips smack hers fast and furious. He tastes like the mac and cheese they had for lunch.

Myrna's body is confused. There's a lot going on, a lot involved. Best called the Wanderer for its habit of veering off in unplanned directions and winding up lost, Myrna's vagus nerve travels through her organs, picking up secrets and spreading gossip. The self-proclaimed Know-It-All in her brain and the Idiot Savant bobbing in her stomach acid would never communicate if it weren't for the Wanderer. All life's major decisions, regardless of what people would like to believe, are made by these three.

At the animal scent of Paul, Myrna's brain sparks. Her skin registers his body heat, and happy hormones race through her blood. But in the mediated conversation between the Know-It-All and the Idiot Savant, the message changes. Euphoria morphs into something closer to repulsion, a firm backing away. In the fermenting nether regions, where essential nutrients are put to use throughout the body, an unavoidable sense of something terribly wrong announces itself, and Myrna shuts down.

This is the first boy who's ever shown interest. Mama would be so proud for her girl to find a handsome boy. A week later, Myrna and Paul can be witnessed walking the school hallways arm-in-arm. Boyfriend and girlfriend, they're officially going steady.

· 7 ·

At her prom, Myrna stands against the cold wall, watching. She's wearing the purple orchid Paul bought her over the left breast of the green velvet dress Mama made. Her hair is parted at the side and pulled back by an antique gold comb that used to be Baba's. Her face itches from the foundation Mama slathered on. The two of them crowded into the only bathroom in the house for a tedious hour, Mama intent on her mission, Myrna watching her small face in the mirror once again becoming a person she does not know.

The graduates have had their prime rib, and she wants to

go home, put on sweatpants and dream up movie plots with her boyfriend. Those moments are when they're best, not now in the banquet hall with the disco ball throwing stars over the parquet and girls in bodice-shaping gowns doing moves with guys in satin shirts and wide-bottomed pants.

Paul invites her to dance, but she tells him no, and he doesn't pressure. She sees him doing the bump with a well-curved girl, the almost delicate way he rubs against her, the open hunger on his square face, and she wants him to enjoy himself.

The students party to the end of high-school conformity, although few besides Myrna are likely to describe the sense of freedom with quite those words. Some plan to work a while and travel. Many of the grads are going away for school.

When Myrna gets into professional motion picture production at the local technical college, her Mama is overcome with pride. Myrna's one of only two females in the new program.

· 8 ·

Whenever she gets in front of the editing table, the instructor finds a reason to rub his hairy forearm with the linked watchband across her breasts. On the pretense of helping her learn, he lingers close and cops a feel, coming in from the right when she marks a frame. If she inches away, he edges his chair closer, the rubber stoppers squeaking over the linoleum floor.

Once he's stolen feels, all the boys feel welcome. The stares and the brushing up are bad, worse is the boy who, one day, cups a breast when the instructor has stepped out of the classroom. She's waiting her turn at the editing table, he's standing beside her when, without any warning, he plucks her breast. Like a ripe grapefruit, her holds her in his palm. She pretends it's a joke, laughter sputtering through her lips, fast and lethal as bullets to the faces of those who think his behaviour is entertaining. Then she jabs his guts hard with the sharpness of her elbow. He groans and backs away.

If getting time at the editing table is difficult, laying hands on the Bolex is nearly impossible. Precision-made and reliable, the camera offers power. When she removes the Bolex from the equipment room without properly signing it out during the equipment monitor's coffee break, mere hours from the end of classes on Friday afternoon, she knows the responsibility she's taking.

· 9 ·

Inside the security vestibule with the overhead camera and the huge, dark panel of glass, a woman's voice comes from above like God, and Myrna explains why she's there. She doesn't know whether it's the hush in her voice that convinces them or the wild fear in her eyes. It's a miracle they let her in. She's imagined more than once what it'd be like to need a place like this. They have strict security. It's a female underground railroad without any tracks. It took serious sleuthing to find the location.

Seems to Myrna she should use power for something that matters, and this is what she tells the two staff members gathered in the small office with no windows. They allow her to enter the second-stage shelter for battered women and their children. She'd hoped for half an hour; they give her a full afternoon. She promises to give the staff the last say on content. Fresh-skinned Leah with the small mouth and silent baby, grey-haired Bandi with the snuffed-out eyes, Cheryl with the teeth-grinding laugh—Myrna would not do anything to harm them.

Later, the instructor who'd taken liberties admits her footage is stunning, powerful, and bold. Her doc wins first place at the Festival of Short Films. Free as they felt to touch her, none of her classmates wanted to work on the project. They didn't see Myrna as director material, a production assistant, maybe. She longs to work with Paul again. She thinks of him often when she's filming, even make-believes debates they'd have. They still exchange intimate letters, although they both know the romance is over.

· 10 ·

Myrna remembers the exact moment. She'd been standing in the dining room at the shelter. It could've been a high-school cafeteria, what with the off-white tables and grey folding chairs, except the room wasn't filled with teenagers but with women and children who were not safe at home. Inside her camera, Myrna held their stories, yet she couldn't help feeling some awkwardness when offered their hugs. The floor-to-ceiling windows open to a fenced green lawn monitored by police security cameras.

And there is Alice, waiting for everybody else to say goodbye to Myrna before she steps forward. Wearing baby-blue cotton baggy pants rolled at the bottom and fastened to the waist with a fat white belt. She'd been one of the first counsellors Myrna interviewed. Her wild black curls are unharnessed, a pure mayhem of frizz and twirl and glorious volume. She's got pink hoop earrings and a sprinkling of freckles over her nose.

When it's finally their turn, they begin a conversation that lasts so long that by the time they part, the dining room is deserted. Only the two of them remain, embraced in conversation in the slanted light of early evening. Alice has finished her shift. She doesn't have to rush back to work.

"I love the wilderness, especially the mountains. A glacial turquoise lake . . ."

"In a two-person canoe, late afternoon cooling . . . loons calling."

"Wearing long sleeves and full pants due to the bugs and also the sun. A goofy straw hat, rock-star shades."

"Taking sips of Chianti straight from the bottle . . ."

"Nibbling blue cheddar . . ."

"And ripping chunks off a fresh baguette, passing the loaf back and forth, trying not to tip over. . . ."

Myrna blushes to be seen and heard, a full-body assurance of safety and comfort, such sweet precious comfort. Her heartbeat settles, and her guts sink into a warm bath. The Idiot Savant floats, one hand at the back of the neck, the other pressed to the belly button, knees wide in butterfly, feet joined. Meanwhile, Know-It-All has already tallied the indicators, churned through scenarios, declared it love. Dashing back and forth, the Wanderer is kept busy spreading the good news to all the vital organs.

· 11 ·

In Mama's familiar kitchen, Myrna watches the lesson unfold. The pretty black canisters with red roses line up against the yellow-tiled backsplash. Each area of the grey-speckled countertop is designated for a specific task. Her lover and her mother are working together. Alice is learning to mix dough by feel, to tuck it under a checkered tea towel for a rest, to roll it smooth and cut it into a perfect grid with a butter knife.

Soon after they met, Alice told Myrna about her parents. She'd waited until she was twenty-one and felt she could no longer hide who she was. But the small O of her mother's mouth, the choked sobs. And the rising up of her father. Fundamentalist Christians, they believed there can be no other union before God but that between a man and his wife. Alice knew she was no longer held. She knew she was no longer safe. In all the years since, she hadn't spoken to either of her parents.

So, when Mama seems to catch the very sorrow in Alice's sad mouth, Myrna doesn't understand how that could happen. She has trouble believing it's real. She'd delayed introductions because she knew it'd be hard, not only for Alice. Myrna has yet to tell her own parents what they must already guess.

She and Alice have been dating a year. They are planning to move in together, and this is the first time Mama and Alice have met. And yet, somehow, Mama takes hold of the loneliness in Alice's tucked chin. She notices Alice's hesitation to come near. And, being Mama, she does the only thing she knows how to do for a downcast girl. She welcomes Alice into the kitchen and teaches her to make pierogies.

The matryoshka dolls stand in line, stages of woman-hood watching. Alice looks so contented pinching closed the pierogies Mama fills. Mama brushes an unruly black curl out of Alice's eyes. They both get flour smudged on their noses. See, thinks Myrna, each doll fits within another, but the swaddled baby is loved by all. When Alice says she'd like to be the one to get pregnant, Myrna understands.

· 12 ·

At weddings, the older relatives whisper to Mama, "When are you going to do something about your girl?" Mama has six siblings, which makes for a lot of weddings and a whole lot of females worried for Myrna's future. By this time, Myrna is thirty, and people are starting to panic.

Rumours spread in ladies' washrooms where relatives gather to freshen their lipstick. With the hushed voices come laments. "Such as waste, such a sadness," they say. "Poor Mama, she'll never get grand-kiddies."

They don't know Myrna and Alice hiked four hours in the company of a fast-flowing river with water white as mother's milk, through a brave pine forest and rocky terrain to reach the Twin Falls. They don't know that the night before their nuptials, Myrna stayed in a wilderness lodge at the base of said falls. Nor do they know that, as the sun moved down the valley, the two women hiked farther to the very mouth of the falls, where they sat on a high shelf next to the two mighty streams at the exact point where they each blast free over a cliff to be joined at the bottom below. Perfectly capable of sealing their own covenant, they'd married themselves three months before Myrna's thirtieth birthday. A little older, Alice is thirty-five when they take their vows.

· 13 ·

Myrna stacks dirty dishes by the sink, Mama scrubs them clean, and Alice dries. Frugal her whole life, Mama is not the sort of woman who buys a dishwasher. She doesn't believe a machine could ever get things as clean as her own two hands.

Every daughter wants to be cared for, to belong, to be cherished. Mama wrapped her arms around Alice, and neither Alice nor Myrna could let go. The couple in love acquiesced to boundaries of intimacy whenever they were with Myrna's parents. Sitting close on the couch was okay; holding hands was not. It was absurd, really. There'd only ever been one bed in the apartment they share, and neither parent asked why.

Once they've taken care of the other dishes. Mama drags the silver-framed chair-and-stool-in-one to the section of cupboards where her best dishes are stored. Myrna loves the blue marble vinyl on the seat and the back of the chair. Such things can no longer be found in any store.

Mama carefully stacks the porcelain teacups she inherited from Baba on the top shelf. The teacups are reserved for special occasions like Sunday dinners with her best girls.

Myrna feels Baba near every time she reaches for the delicate handle of a teacup. A flood of memories, tender moments as a troublesome girl with unruly hair, calmed in the presence of Baba. They'd have their own private tea party on a dull weekend afternoon using the hand-painted orange and yellow and blue flowered teacups, the saucers ringed with clusters of berries on the vine.

"Mama, there's something we have to tell you." In that moment, Myrna knows she stands alone now. Although she came out of Mama, and Mama came out of Baba, she is apart now. It is like her middle bears the mark from where she was split in half and re-joined as a distinct person.

"I love Alice, Mama. She is my only one. We're going to spend the rest of our lives together as married as any couple. Can you accept that?"

The teacups rattle. Mama shuts the cupboard door. She steps down from the stool, looking first at Myrna and then Alice. "Guess you can't help what you are," she says, wiping her mouth, swallowing. "I still love you."

Myrna presses her hip to Alice's side. Their fingers interlock.

"Fine, then. Okay," says Mama, pulling a tissue from the big pocket on her yellow checkered apron. "We don't ever need speak of this again. But don't tell me I can't be sad. No grandchildren. Every mama wants grandchildren."

When Mama turns from them and goes to her bedroom, shutting the door without saying goodnight, Myrna and Alice are still holding hands.

· 14 ·

All is hushed in the moderately sized bathroom with its ultra-white, high-gloss walls, black floor tiles and silvery marbled countertop. The vanity had a worn oak finish until Myrna covered it with grey chalk paint and a smoky glaze. They'd squeezed a retro vanity stool with a red and white striped cushion and curled metal legs into the unused corner.

Myrna is perched on the stool. Alice is on the throne. They are waiting. Three years of trying, five different male friends or friends-of-friends, a weakening of romance within the ongoing science experiment of conception, and an unyielding yearning. The oval window on the white stick laid flat on the silvery marbled countertop shows two clear blue lines. They lean in and kiss and are overcome with giggles.

Eight weeks later, Alice is on the examining table in the fresh medical office with all those clean surfaces gleaming with happiness. A kindly young woman with bright teeth puts gel on the round end of a thick wand. Alice's blue paper gown is open, her swollen breasts no longer fit the bra, and she is buzzing. When Myrna, standing on the opposite side of the table, reaches out and takes Alice's hand, she feels the charge like a hum in her own nerves.

The sonographer moves the wand this way and that, pressing into the belly flesh, pausing to look at the screen. In the static, the women do not know what they are looking for.

"Excuse me," says the sonographer, resting a hand briefly on Alice's shoulder, avoiding her eyes. "Be right back. Just need to talk to the doctor for a moment."

After the sonographer leaves them alone, Myrna and Alice are no longer buzzing. All is deadly silent now. Five minutes later, they're given the news—the sack is empty.

A fertilized egg implanted in the uterus did not develop into an embryo. All the signs of pregnancy, celebration of the new life they'd nurture together, and the medical world say none of it was real.

· 15 ·

Three more years of bitter effort ends with Alice in the hospital tucked between blue sheets with a faded white blanket on top. The piss-yellow curtains are drawn around her bed. The staff have finally left them alone.

Since the first of their losses, Myrna has hauled herself around, making documentaries, acting like nothing is wrong for the sake of Alice. But her nose and throat are shivery, and there's a squeeze around her heart. Everyone else gets their dreams of family and children, and she and Alice must carry theirs around dead. The unborn. It is not fair.

She never means to pull away, but the pain in her heart, it makes Myrna tender. And true to her word, Mama never mentions their relationship at the Sunday dinners that march on endlessly. The couple knows better than to confide in Mama or Papa what they cannot bear between them.

When Alice carries past ten weeks for the very first time, hope festers around Myrna's heart. She thickens with a dare-not-dream infection and is helpless to stop the spread. They delay the ultrasound, an event that has brought only heartache every other time.

They're watching a wretched-excess TV series about manu-facturing illegal drugs, lost for a while in someone else's suffer-ing. Halfway through the episode, Alice presses a hand to her not-yet-showing belly and cries out, "Ouch. Ow. That really hurts."

The ambulance comes minutes later. Alice loses consciousness en route and has not come to when she arrives at the hospital. They don't allow Myrna to go with her as they wheel the stretcher full-speed down the busy hallway. This time a fetus grew, but in her Fallopian tube, expanding cell by cell until it split the tube wide open. Alice almost died from internal bleeding. If Myrna had hesitated to call 9–1–1, Alice might no longer be alive.

This is a loss Myrna had not considered, the absence of her one. Into that ache, she presses all of herself that remains, carefully placing herself on the too-small hospital bed, curling an arm over Alice's shoulder, kissing her freckled cheeks, wiping away tears.

In the hallways, nurses roll their carts. Visitors bring gifts of flowers and books to their friends and relatives.

Shush, be quiet. Shut up and listen, says the Wanderer. *This is now*, whispers Know-It-All, properly humbled on her knees. And Idiot Savant, she inhales sharply, pauses into the great dark, unknown chill, and with a very long sigh, lets go.

"Alice, my love. I am here. We will figure this out. Together."

· 16 ·

They name her Kaylila, which means one who is loved. Born to a mother over forty, the effort was high-risk. Three short years after, she does what Mama declared impossible, Myrna stops menstruating. Alice goes another five.

But their sweetest toddler with green eyes and curly black hair pinned back by a barrette shaped like a starfish makes such markers less significant. After the birth of her grandchild, Mama brings her knuckles to her forehead and says sorry. Papa doesn't fuss, although it's doubtful he ever really understands, and he dies of a stroke a year after his grandchild is born.

By four months, Kaylila can sit on her own, her roly-poly thighs settled low, her knees spread wide. By five months, she can roll from one side of the room to the other at ferocious speed. And by eight months, holy wow, she can crawl, bum high and arms straight, drooling.

Round about eleven months, Kaylila is ready to try walking. Cruising from one parent to the other, she keeps three-point contact, two feet on the floor and a hand on the strong surface of a mama's knee. If ever she loses her balance, she sticks out her bum and pauses on wobbly feet, then self-corrects with a tuck of the hips. Progress is gradual. When she lands on her bum, her mamas take turns helping their child onto her feet, holding her hands gently from behind, letting her find her own balance.

The first time Kaylila stays afloat, she's making a trip from Myrna to Alice. Standing bow-legged, she looks anything but steady. Ever so slowly, she loosens her right foot and swings it forward. The stubby foot lands. Her arms reach for balance, palms flat as if over the surface of water. Her left foot swings forward. With two more steps, Kaylila falls into one of her mama's arms. Seconds later, Kaylila is enveloped from behind.

Intimacy

David steps through the front door and sets down his briefcase. He takes off his double-breasted jacket and tweed scarf. He unties his grey oxfords and sets his feet free with a sigh.

Lynn hears the door and lifts her chef's knife. With careful precision, she chops the garlic into fine pieces.

In the dead air of their living room, the late afternoon sun glares over the dusty coffee table with nothing on it. He looks at the overstuffed brown leather armchair where he spends most evenings alone now. The seat is beginning to sag.

She dabs the inch-thick rib-eye with a paper towel and cracks sea salt and black pepper over the raw meat. The cut was chosen for its tenderness. Massive as it is, she thought they might share the single steak, that it would be in some way romantic.

He wonders, if he asked, would she agree to spend time with

him after dinner? Would she nuzzle next to him, even briefly? They could start with that, maybe.

She adds hot salted water to her thickening risotto. After a light stir of the puddly concoction, she tosses sliced mushrooms into a pan of melted butter.

Standing lost in his own home, David picks up the faint scent of caramelized onion from earlier in the risotto making, the sharpness turned sweet. Unmet longing seeps into his flesh. It draws him to her.

The thick hunk of marbled meat lands on the slick surface of the smoking-hot pan. A satisfying sizzle rises from beneath the cold beef. Silvery wisps of smoke waft around the fatty edges.

He waits at the entrance to their modern kitchen with stark white cupboards and black countertops. He hesitates in stocking feet.

"Hello, dear," she says without turning. "Welcome home." She slides the long-handled pan back and forth, tossing the mushrooms, taking care to coat every slice. That's the only reason she doesn't greet him like a proper wife. Later, in a minute, she tells herself.

He joins her at the stove. Cupping her shoulder, he leans over her mushrooms. "Smells good. I'm starving." To the side, he sees the gently simmering risotto and thick steak. She's really putting herself out.

She sets down the pan on the burner and turns towards him. The flat of her palm presses his heart, and she draws closer. Their lips meet in a swirl of body warmth and sweat and shared breath, their long life together. Everything will be okay, she thinks, if only she tries.

Briefly, he finds salvation, the single act of affection atoning for whatever sins they have committed upon each other. He no longer cares. It's been near on eight months since they've had physical intimacy. And now, it seems his decision to wait for her lead was the best way out of their dead pass.

Lynn brings to the table one rice bowl of glistening risotto for each of them, creamed-over joy garnished with zest of lemon and finely chopped chives. The plates have already been served. She stood back and adjusted each to its proper centre before he sat down. The plummy Malbec, which mates perfectly, has been poured. She puts herself in place, unfolding the napkin over her lap, patting it down.

Before marriage and her job as an instructor, before she'd sold her soul for security, Lynn did as she'd pleased, not knowing how lucky she'd been. A freelance photographer, she'd spent hours arranging food and lights and taking photos. Entire days wasted shooting silly things like coffee bean shadows.

David would not disturb the quivering surface of her risotto. He's reluctant to touch anything on his plate, to spoil what she's done for him. He knows she's not happy as an instructor. The cucumber ribbons are loosely spooled and stood on end, their dark green lines and glass-like flesh drizzled in honey and lemon and dill. And the sliced steak, pink in the middle, she's layered over a warm bed of mushrooms. Mint leaves and deep orange nasturtium petals are scattered at the edges of the square white plates.

He reaches across the table and pats her hand. "This looks amazing. You've outdone yourself." Her fair cheeks are flushed, her green eyes intense, and her lips are slightly moist and parted.

"Oh, this?" she says. "It's nothing." She does not welcome the sour thoughts, how her mouth puckers at the creative energy laid out on the dazzling white plates. The wasted time arranging food only to be eaten.

With the sharp points of her fork, she tears down the cucumber spirals, moves the steak out of place, messes up the orange petals. There now, better. At first, she does not realize he has been watching.

Armed with fork and knife, he furtively studies the woman he calls wife. He does not want to upset her, and there's still a chance this might work. But in recent weeks, he's gained some distance from their problems, enough at least to question her intentions. He's begun to notice that thing she does where she quashes any small helping of joy they might've shared.

"I wanted to do something special for you," she says before taking a lingering sip of the rich wine. From above the tilted wine glass, she waits for his reaction.

"Thank you," he gulps, regretting his unkind thoughts. "I'm enjoying this," he adds with enthusiasm. "It's been too long since you and I shared a romantic dinner."

He cuts into the pink flesh and brings the first bite to his mouth. The meal is exactly right, balanced to heighten his pleasure, tasty. His teeth grind the flesh, releasing its juices. She's watching him now, and his lips rub in pleasure.

She, too, has been considering. Mr. V.P. Academic is a busy man, too busy actually to come to the hospital and support his wife as her mother lay dying. They work at the same campus, it's how they met, and she knows all that he's responsible for. And still, she does not think it was right how she'd endured the loss of her only parent completely alone in the cold dingy hospital.

He blames her long back with the inward curve, her delicate shoulders and her willowy arms, how she moves like a dancer. After their meal, he transfers the leftover risotto, which is clumpier now it's cold, into a glass container with a snap-over lid. In their marriage, he clears, and she cleans. It's their way.

He steps gingerly towards her back at the kitchen sink. When he leans in and presses his lips to the sensitive spot behind her ear, she's not expecting him. His chin must be bristly and rough, he worries. And still, he blunders on. In his best sexy voice, growly with lust, he whispers close to her ear tenderly, "Couldn't wait, sweetheart."

A shiver rings through her spine, reverberating in her bones. She holds it quiet, her flesh a muffle to the sound, the inner trembling. Rubber-gloved, she turns off the tap. He's a man with normal needs. The greasy pan sinks into the soapy water. "Oh, my dearest. I've missed you too."

Encouraged, he reaches for her hips, his thumbs hooking her waist. As she turns around to face him, out of the twist knot that keeps her hair under control, an auburn curl escapes. It plays at the side of her face, a reminder of lighter-hearted days when he'd tug her away from the sink, and she'd pretend to resist, and it would increase their mutual pleasure. If only they could be loving again, he believes, their marriage would recover.

Except under the broad chest, the successful career in academia, he is ashamed of how he failed her. She'd called to him as her mother lay dying. It does no good to explain—the funding meeting in the capital, three years of programs at risk, the ferocious winter storm he could not control, and the impassable highway conditions, cars jammed in the mesmerizing madness of windblown icy snow.

She takes comfort in what they've shared, the known fact of their love. He smells of the sandalwood aftershave she bought him for Christmas. She'd do anything to take back the way her shoulder clenched when he gave her a playful kiss. Does he know she, too, remembers how they used to be?

With wide hands, he draws her in, presses close to his own bruising, to the smell of her sweat, to his sorrow. Overcome by the warmth emanating from her body, the sweet curve of her shoulders, the way she smells, he blames himself for what happens next. If only he'd allowed her to lead, maybe they might have found their way.

She clings to his back, which would have been good, except her hands are fierce, and her mouth freezes under the insistence of his.

Lynn knows she is not welcoming, leaning back over the sink. She knows David's interest will surely not endure. She smooches him back, allows a low moan to fill her throat, remembers when that sound only announced their most intimate moments.

The awakening urge in the base of his spine, the warmth in his groin, the pressure building. What they need, he thinks, is a good strong cleansing passion. The mind-melting kind, the moment of salvation kind, the tingly outburst and now I can rest kind. She is here, and she is kissing him. "Shall we go upstairs?" he asks.

"Yes, dear." She eases him away, and her back sings hallelujah, thank goodness that's over. "That would be nice," she murmurs, turning to the dirty pots soaking in cooling water. There is nothing erotic in having your back broken. He'd know that if he'd stopped to think. "Just let me finish here," she adds, and begins scouring a pan, scraping away the caked-on food, holding the pan near water level to watch her progress. "I'll only be a minute."

Was not her touch gentle as she nudged him out of the way? She couldn't continue with her back bent in that awkward position, he's aware. It's not unreasonable to want to take care of domestic chores. Perhaps she needed a clear mind. But does she ever stop and think how this makes him feel? Useless as a man. Unwanted and abandoned. All the time scheming ways to draw her interest. Suppose he chose instead to plunk down in the reliable armchair in their lonely living room and not go to their bedroom at all.

Over his lap, covered by a flannel sheet and downy comforter, the e-book glows. When she arrives in their bedroom, he's propped against a stack of pillows reading. She's asked him before not to rush sex. It's not like he's forgotten. She needs more time to reach arousal, he understands. If she's pressured into intercourse before her body's ready, she told him, the friction rips her apart. They're no longer young, he must not make assumptions, and anyway, he needs more time too if she'd care to ask.

Back turned, she peels off her sweater, steps out of her pants. She unfastens the bra with a sigh before wiggling out of her panties. The cool air makes her shiver up the torso to her shoulders, and next to her heart, deep within, a quivering uncertainty. The left side of her mother's brain, it had gushed blood for days after the massive stroke.

He hears the layers being peeled from her body, the plop as each item lands on the carpet. He recollects the pale innocence of her skin. The wrinkly parts and random dents, he has seen them all before, and the thick folds she perceives as unflattering like handholds above her hip bones. He'd like to watch, and yet, knows that'd be too much, that she needs a strange sort of privacy now even in their bedroom. Instead, he waits until she's ready for him before flipping closed his e-book and tossing the extra pillows onto the floor.

Her mother lay dying after the stroke. She'd been in a coma. There'd been little hope she'd ever wake. And twice, Lynn had heard the most heart-rending moans from her mother's unconscious body. No, she scolds herself. You stop that, right now. Focus on David, who is here now and breathing. Look at him, tucked in and waiting for love.

She puts on the fleshy-toned silk. So floaty-alive, and a fresh part of her, like a second perfect skin. The expensive pyjamas make her feel beautiful. And she slips under the covers next to him in that state, burrowing into their hidden den, seeking animal warmth. Oh, how freely her second skin loves him. He must be relieved for once to not have to encourage her.

Pressing into his body, she listens to his heartbeat, following the rhythm of his breath. She'd spoken to her mother every single day in person or on the phone. A thing hadn't really happened until they'd discussed it.

The silk awakens his skin, every hair on his exposed flesh poking its way upward in delight. He draws her closer with a moan he's helpless to deny.

The creamy, soothing layer gives her freedom. The protection allows her to feel a little, she's noticed. When he rubs the unreachable zone of her upper back in gentle circles, she collapses into him.

And then his hands find other business. Hungrily, he slides a palm down her side and explores beneath the silk until he finds what he wants. "I don't think you'll be needing these," he says, tugging down her pyjama bottoms.

The top slips off a moment later. She feels the silk abandoning her, the rawness of her naked skin, the need to escape. He lays over her. They begin.

"Mom would've liked the risotto," she says, knowing full well the mistake she's making. "It was her recipe, I think."

It's happened so often, the yearning and the restraint, the agony of waiting, the failure. He no longer rushes to kindness and he does not recognize the man who emerges. With straight arms, he hovers over her. Looking down on her cowering face, he shakes his head. "Oh, God," he says. "Can't it ever be the two of us anymore? This is making me crazy."

Unclothed, David stands on the carpet. His hairy legs and his big-toed feet, the tender mouth on his hardened face. She has done this to him, and she knows not how to help. Whatever she might do, it will never be enough. For the first time, she considers the true meaning of kindness. He has left their bed, she is alone now, and the sorrow in his grey eyes makes her hate herself.

"All I need is a little affection. Is that too much to ask?" His throat thickens. She must hear it. But could she ever know, really, how his heart hammers his ribs, as if it might shatter the bars of its cage, as if it might free itself. Such a fool he is to imagine he might draw her back, to not see she is already gone.

The attention, the cocoon of care, all of it unwound and fell away the moment her mother died. An only child and an only parent, this is a closeness David knows nothing of. Lynn was left a raw piece of flesh, completely exposed, as if she had no skin. It hurts now having anyone near. Why can't he understand?

Her sigh is more a shudder as she hauls herself up against the headboard. "I'm sorry," she says slowly. The way his arms hang loose at his sides, the way his fingers open, he is no longer holding onto anything. And it is all her fault that he makes no effort to cover himself.

"What is it you want? Tell me." The sound of his own voice settles him. The insurrection of his heart, it all comes to an end, and the flow of blood through his muscles banishes all of their unshared moments. He takes his housecoat from the chair and wraps it around himself. She does nothing to stop him.

Morning is seeping through the curtains when David hears his wife enter the guest room where he's been trying to sleep. He follows her naked body as she crosses the floor, draws back the covers, and gets in.

She yearns for his touch, to taste his lips, to open to him. This is the first time in years she's felt such a need. She presses against him, runs her fingers through his hair. Maybe it's seeing him in another bed, she tells herself. Or having a choice, it could be that. Or going to him free to leave.

He could've tried to outlast the unwelcome lips against his neck. He could've tried to remember the warmth of her hair over his skin. Suppose he'd offered to wait for the comfort to be found in their nakedness. But his spine locks against her, rigid with defence.

"This is not something that can be fixed by sex," he says, pushing her away.

"We can talk later," she answers.

And on the floor, her feet land tenderly. Hushed, she leaves. Somehow now perfectly at ease unclothed, she does not turn back. In their bedroom, she gets dressed.

Saturday mornings, they like to sleep in, although never this late. He sits in his usual spot, and she pours him fresh coffee. While she mixes the pancake batter and adds a cluster of fresh blueberries, he holds the mug in both hands, staring off into nothing. She finds the stash of real maple syrup at the back of the pantry, shapes butter into a bowl, and places the offerings in front of him.

He would like to see her cry. All the months of sobbing in public after her mother died. Does the loss of their marriage not merit tears? Flittering around the kitchen, making a show of her effort. She no longer needs him, that's what it means. She hasn't needed him for a long time.

Furious now, aware he must seem a child for having a temper tantrum. Pushing his plate away, David says, "Don't give me any more of your damn food. I'm not hungry."

The first time he saw her, she was at the front of a mock classroom, fumbling around, clearly not in her element. Under the powder blue dress, he could see her shoulders quake. At that point, he was academic coordinator. He'd stopped by the workshop to observe briefly. She hadn't taught a real class yet. Her mouth made that clicking sound people get when they're out-of-their-body nervous.

She pushes his plate back to him, surprised by her own actions. Chin up and eyes forward, she's ready now to face him. "Try a little," she says in a gentle voice. "It might help you feel better."

A swirl is building inside her. Not to be unkind, she knows this is awful, but already she's imagining changes she might make. She's begun to see things in a new light. How her mother had renovated the basement in her home, that was not necessarily so generous. Getting her daughter to pay rent, maybe there had been more to that than kindness. Since they'd met, David has been telling her what to do. Maybe she doesn't want to be a bloody instructor.

He picks up a fork and knife, smears butter over a pancake,

douses it in syrup, cuts a small piece and sticks it in his mouth. She is right. It does make him feel better.

She watches him swallow, thinking she's done some little thing for him. Her pancakes are the best, he's told her many times. She's surprised when he does not continue after the first mouthful.

His fork and knife clunk onto the table she'd prettied up with placemats and stupid cloth napkins. The tenderness in his face, it wounds her.

He reaches across the table and squeezes her fingers. "I can't do this anymore," he says. "It hurts too much being near you."

They pack the station wagon together. After they finish loading his stuff, they linger in the driveway. The bright glare off the snow makes Lynn's eyes water.

David's jacket is open. His heart flutters with an unexpected freedom. He no longer has to try. He's wearing the thick grey sweater her mom knitted for him. He knows perfectly well there are bristles on his face. He chose not to shave.

Without thinking, she kisses his cheek. He kisses hers, breathing in the scent of her face cream, yearning in spite of himself, wishing he didn't. They share a final brief embrace before he gets into the station wagon and leaves.

Alone in their house, Lynn takes in a slow breath. Once, twice. Something is broken inside, barbed edges. She must move carefully through the silent rooms.

The potted daffodils on the antique table, the multi-coloured pens blooming from a pottery mug by the phone, the fading light skimming the surface of the countertop, all the details are sharp and bright.

She goes to their bedroom and pulls her camera from the closet. The thick strap over the back of her neck slackens as she raises the lens.

Double Zero

Why do I put myself through the humiliation? Darya asks herself. It's day one of her new life, and already she cannot see one reason she shouldn't quit. Huffing on an exercise bike, set to hill climb, in the crowded exercise room stinking of rubber and other people's sweat. She's not up to the task. Any fool can see that.

It doesn't help that the person who makes her feel most powerless is perched on the next bike. Ms. Wonderful in her designer workout gear, the kind with a flowery strip along the outside of the thighs. She's got a neon pink water bottle and a state-of-the-art MP3 player with purple earbuds. A woman like Ms. Wonderful only works out for show. She doesn't need it, unlike Darya who has more than one spare tire. Divorced with grown children who live too far away to see very often, Darya has only a few tedious encounters with near-strangers for company. Yes, those blind dates arranged by her mother and other women from church. It's been months since she's done even that. But yeah, she has a workout plan.

And she might even accomplish it if she weren't stuck beside the same woman who interrupted her in the staff meeting an hour earlier. Darya has done research on student engagement. She has a grant, okay, and she wanted to share her ideas with colleagues before sharpening her research questions. Ms. Wonderful cut in on the pretense of offering suggestions, when really all she'd wanted was to brag.

Darya looks around. That guy on the thingy with the cables and bars, reaching up with monkey arms, slowly pulling down. Good Lord, save me. How his biceps bulge. And that woman with the uppity ponytail, face down on a bench that only supports her legs, supplicating with her hands crossed over her chest, slowly bowing. People like that make Darya feel useless.

She'd be gone if it weren't for the grey-haired chick on the bike at her other side. Now, that's a real woman. Darya is drawn to the confidence, the I-do-not-give-an-F attitude, and how the woman sweats like an animal.

Darya has no interest in a dainty waist, and she can do without perky breasts. What she wants and needs is power, kicking legs, a rock-hard abdomen, a nice impenetrable shield. She's too squooshy around the middle. People assume she won't fight back. She's been shoved around her whole career, pathetic, really. Thirty years of working at the college, and she hasn't advanced once. She's in the same job they hired her for: junior instructor.

Turning to the grey-haired chick, clearing her throat, Darya croaks, "Excuse me." Where does she think she is? Skipping ahead in line at the movie theatre? What a ridiculous thing to say. She's got to have more in her. Above the din of exercise machines and disco, she bellows it out. "Holy bananas. You're working hard."

The woman's wearing sweatpants and a plain grey t-shirt, nothing designer there. Wet marks spread around the neck of her shirt and under her armpits. She turns to Darya, her legs keeping pace. "Yeah, well . . . I'm here . . . so I might as well really be here. Know what I mean?"

A wicked grin fills the woman's face as her eyes shift to the other side of Darya. This could not get any better. Ms. Wonderful is holding a magazine in sweat-free hands, her legs engaged in near-effortless pedalling. They both know who the "being here" comment is about.

"If I wanted a rest," adds the real athlete, "I'd go someplace with less noise."

They are bonded, two sincere people in a room full of fakers and show-offs. Darya feels the other woman's strength taking over. Watch me go. Wow. Oh, lady. Darya stomps down and pulls up, repeats, each time with more effort. Adrenaline is its own kind of drug. Her heart and lungs scream at the madness, but her legs are possessed. Never mind the burn on her face, the scraped-away feeling at the back of her throat, the deeply rooted sense of an impending crash. The encased wheel inside the machine whirls.

Maria appreciates an honest try when she sees one, and the woman on the bike next to hers certainly earned a shower. She does not fail to pick up on the woman's enthusiasm, the way she hangs on every word, the glossy-eyed adoration. From a different source, it might have seemed patronizing, but when Maria looks at the woman's butt slopping over the bike seat, she sees herself a year earlier.

Back then, she was muffin-topped too, coated in more padding than her pants could contain. That was before the truth knocked her breathless and insisted she reach inside for inner strength, or give up the ghost and be done with it. She caught her wife kissing someone else on a quiet stretch of the river pathway. She'd only wanted to clear her head after too many hours shopping. It was the week before Christmas and, as usual, Maria had overspent.

The fresh creature taking kisses from Maria's wife had perfect skin and the shiniest copper hair. Thinking back, Maria figures it was probably dyed. Seriously, there was nothing natural about that colour. The woman was wearing a long royal blue jacket and a snowy white hat, looking for all the world like a Russian princess. And Maria's wife? How dare she? Sammy came off top-class in her smartly tailored tweed jacket, the one they'd picked out together on their trip to Ireland last summer. Big snowflakes wafted down under a darkening sky. *Isn't that romantic*, thought Maria, before registering what the beautifully designed organs that are her eyes wanted to tell her fool of a brain.

Because yes, oh mother, it's true. Bodies are hopelessly stupid things. If a person doesn't teach their body a thing or two, it will happily pursue its own destruction, wrapping its middle in fat, smothering vital organs. A body will run from the truth, panting down an icy pathway, nearly falling on its face, feet sliding everywhere. And later at home, the same body will tidy itself up and float around the house in its best festive dress, the red one with a fake white-fur collar. At bedtime, it will leave the lamp on, and it will let warm hands cup its breasts. Then, sure enough, it will flop like a dead fish into a naked hug, its brain silenced in advance by a strong club to the head. She'd stayed with Sammy for months after discovering the infidelity, acting as if nothing was wrong.

On the way back to work, Darya spots the inspiring woman up ahead. She elbows her way through the throng of students. Suddenly brutal with determination, she manages to catch up. When Maria sees her, she shifts over to make room.

"I'm Darya," she blurts. Oh yeah, that's a great conversation starter. "Really admired your focus back there. Any tips?" Go ahead and make it worse, you idiot.

"Five days a week," says Maria. "At least forty-five minutes of cardio . . . or it won't be enough. Fat burning doesn't kick in until after twenty minutes. So many people don't realize that."

They're walking at a brisk pace, much faster than Darya is used to. Their exercise bags are swinging. Come on, don't be a coward. "Would you consider helping me? I have a plan, but it doesn't say anything about forty-five minutes. It says ten minutes of cardio, then some weights. It's okay if you'd rather not." They cross the stone courtyard and climb the steps to the sandstone hall.

"Same time tomorrow. I'll be there." Maria holds open the big heavy door, thick slats of wood with wrought iron braces and hinges, arched on the top like the entrance to a castle. "You can join me if you want."

Inside the hall, executives have their offices. A coffee shop greets students en route to classes. Don't go and ruin it now. She already said yes. Darya worries that maybe she will not be able to keep up, that they'll try, and she'll fail.

She feels Maria's hand at the back of her arm, nudging her off to the side, a quieter spot away from the onslaught of overcoats and backpacks and elbows. "Trust me," Maria says in a hushed voice. "I understand better than you think."

Darya is not used to people who draw closer, to whispered secrets. She leans in.

"A year ago, I weighed thirty pounds more." Maria smooths the front of her loose black-felt jacket. "Look at me now . . . not perfect, but improving." She pulls up the strap of her exercise bag, which has started to slide off her shoulder. "If you want," she adds with a serious look on her face, "I could show you how."

The next morning, Maria waltzes into the staff locker room, wearing her workout gear under the black-felt coat, carrying her work clothes in an exercise bag, which is her habit. Why change twice? That's her thinking. Plus, to be perfectly honest, she's not a fan of dressing in front of other people.

Darya is ready and waiting. What a keener. She's sitting on the metal bench, gripping the edge.

"Hey, good morning," Maria booms. "And wow, aren't you the early riser?"

With a jolt, Darya stands up, a sudden flush of crimson rising up her neck, a bit like a rash or a hot flash maybe. The poor woman stammers a little, "Ya, yah, ha . . . I've always liked mornings. Hello yourself."

They do an awkward high-five, Maria holding up her hand and waiting, Darya grinning at the clapping sound their palms make when they meet mid-air.

Cute, thinks Maria. She's wearing a t-shirt, check it out, plus proper loose-fitting sweatpants. On the bench rests her water bottle, and it's already filled. Plus, she brought one of those idiotic miniature coiled notebooks and a special thin pen.

Maria flattens her lips before speaking. "You won't be needing that," she says, pointing to the notebook. "My system's simpler. You won't believe how straightforward all of this actually is."

Darya tosses the notebook into her locker and fastens the padlock.

A fat bubble of joy swells Maria's rib cage as she leads them out of the locker room. Isn't it fun how Darya doesn't argue or complain? It feels good to be trusted. It feels right.

They start on the ellipticals. Good thing they're amongst the first to arrive in the exercise room because those wind-up toys are popular amongst fitness enthusiasts. People like the idea that they're using their whole body, arms and legs. Except most people set the tension so low, they might as well be prancing about doing interpretative dance.

Maria sets her machine, and Darya follows suit, carefully dialling it in. Arm up, opposite leg down, stepping up the mountain, graceful and deliberate. Look how Darya mirrors my every move, thinks Maria. Finally, somebody gets it.

"So here's the thing you need to know," Maria tells her companion, already breathing hard. "It works for everything, weights or cardio, and it is stupidly simple. Work as hard as you almighty can . . . then do more. Do that well, and you won't ever need another notebook."

Forty-five minutes later, wet spots on their t-shirts, they are both red in the face. When other people look their way, they ignore them.

Maria and Darya have just enough time to leverage the heat of their muscles. Not many people use the mats in the cramped space set aside for ab work. People prefer the mechanical chair that folds their body in half over their lap with their chest held in place by foam-covered hooks over each shoulder. What is it about people? They think if there's a machine, they're working their muscles more. But have they ever paid attention to the core?

Get real, would ya? If you're working the core, you feel it! An ache inside the ribs, a burn if you're really trying. Do enough variations on crunches using proper form, and you will learn how the strings are strung, the vital bracing that keeps us from falling on our faces, our fail-safe inner system. Some ab muscles run up and down, others crossways.

Bless her, but Darya doesn't give up; that much is absolutely indisputable. She really wants to learn. They lay down their mats side-by-side, so they can see each other. Like synchronized swimmers doing floor exercises. Maria counts them in, "One, begin. Two, engage the core. Three, lift. Four, lower slowly."

Three reps in, Darya confesses, "I have no idea what you're talking about. How do I know whether I have engaged my core?"

So they stop doing crunches for a few minutes. Who cares if they're a little late for work? This is important. Darya needs an inner safety system, same as anyone.

Maria shows her new friend pelvic tilts. She glances over, sees Darya has her eyes closed, does not need to ask. She can feel it in the silence, the two of them together, humbling themselves in a bodily form of prayer.

The thrill in Darya's voice, it is delicious. "Oh, that!" she says. "I get it."

Darya used to tell herself it was second-rate fabric that made her pants accordion at the top of her thighs. And her underpants, they slipped into the crack because the manufacturer cheaped out on fabric. The waistband of her skirt folded whenever she sat down because the twits who made the skirt never bothered using interfacing.

Three months with Maria, and Darya has clothes that fit. She's getting asked on dates, not set-ups by her mom. Currently, she's juggling two might-be-good-enough-for-now possibilities. And, hot damn, if she doesn't put little Ms. Wonderful in her place. The next time that self-important show-off interrupts her, Darya sits up in her chair, her fist lands on the board table in a great big *ka-thump*. "Excuse me, I was talking," she says.

She doesn't need to check their faces. Such silence in the dingy, dark basement meeting room with the four School of Communication instructors and their dean slumped in the ergonomically incorrect chairs in front of the laminate board table with chips along the edges.

"You've heard that the best way to learn something is to teach it." That gets their interest. "Well, it works for students too." Darya hands out photocopies of the main article on which her study is founded. "Peer learning has been used lots of times for problems in math and engineering, or practical skills in medicine, but what about business writing? I'd like to schedule a meeting with anyone willing to contribute ideas. Together, we'll sharpen the research questions. I'm sure you've heard I won a significant grant."

Robert in his toupee and Gloria (aka Ms. Wonderful) in her rose-coloured dress start to read the article with proper attention. Theo with the thick beard says, "Count me in." And Jules the dean in the brow-line glasses, well, she proclaims, "This is good."

Darya can hardly wait to tell Maria, but she knows better than to distract them from their workout. She waits until they're wiping off after an intense session of weights and crunches. They share a towel. And finally, Darya gets to give Maria a play-by-play of the changes in her life. She doesn't skip a thing, hardly stopping enough to breathe. And when she's done, for a minute, there is nothing.

Then Maria says, "Ah, yeah, good for you."

Holy crap, that's all. Really?

"I was thinking tomorrow we should run. Not outside because our pace would not be steady. Inside on treadmills. We'll do intervals."

Darya had been tempted to raise her voice and repeat herself, to stare down the woman who claimed to be her friend. Didn't Maria understand how important this is? Then she let it sink into her ripped abs, the locus of her control, and she knew the reason. Maria is an admin assistant, she's never taught a single class, and she's intimidated by stuff she could never understand.

Anybody can get a decent exercise plan off the internet, Maria has bookmarked dozens, and the idea of working harder isn't revolutionary. Ask any athlete and they'll tell you. Persistence is the only real talent.

She loves the grin on Darya's face when they crank out ten extra crunches, the slap of their palms after they add ten pounds to their dead lifts. They do things other women are afraid to try. After Maria gets back to her desk each morning, she jots down their progress in a notebook she keeps in the top drawer of her desk.

At first, she's careful to limit her sharing to what she knows about exercise. A person can only add so many good habits at once. Darya is doing well. Exercise is absolutely the best foundation, for sure. Start with some muscle, great plan. Thing is though—and nobody wants to admit this—exercise is not enough.

Sooner or later, anyone who is serious figures this out. The first time she and Darya meet for lunch and a fresh course of new skills, Darya is an innocent. "Why's everything cut so small? Oh, those cucumber slices are beautiful . . . like glass almost."

If a person wants the body they deserve, sooner or later, they must fix their relationship with food. And not in the way people think. It's not about depriving yourself of the pleasure of eating. No, the trick is to savour every mouthful that crosses your tongue.

She might have continued as clueless as the rest if it weren't for her wife. In that one way, Sammy had helped her. Their Christmas tree was down. The festivities were good and over. They'd had their fill of empty calories and fake intimacy, pretending to kiss and hold hands and make love. They were no longer interested in gravy and stuffing, would have pushed away shortbread.

Sammy made chili-infused squash soup. They sat across the oval teak table in their fancy chairs with the curved backs. Before the first taste entered her mouth, Maria spat out what was bothering her.

"I saw you before Christmas. On the pathway, necking with a flimsy broad who has cheap copper hair and an expensive velvet coat. You were wearing the tweed jacket we picked out together. What the hell, Sammy?"

"I know ... I'm sorry. We saw you running away ... I've been scared to discuss it. But Maria, sweetheart, swear to God, it was a mistake. A middle-aged identity crisis. A brief lapse in judgment. It's over, I promise. I'll never do anything like that ever again."

A quiet path in the snow, a skinny young thing and her wife acting like she had a different life than the one they'd shared for thirty years. Maria brought a teaspoon of spicy squash to her lips, letting it drain into her mouth. The sweetness and the heat and the joy—all of it was hers and hers alone.

A month later, when she saw a hickey on the neck of her wife that she'd not put there, Maria blinked twice, changing the image, and kissed Sammy on the other side.

Before Maria, Darya doubts she'd ever really tasted her food. A dice-sized cube of smoked gouda could bring a whole mouth alive. A penny-sized cube of dark chocolate was like falling in love, the exact moment of it, the intensity and the rush.

They meet every day for lunch in a quiet corner of the campus, a tiny neglected public space with two small round tables in the basement of the trades building. She and Maria lean close and linger. Together they nibble bits of tart apple, crunch slivers of carrot, drop glassy slices of cold cucumber onto their tongues.

Darya fills with an intense energy, a hum on the inside, a lithe and weightless grace. Colours have become more vivid, the tender green in freshly opened leaves, the golden undertones on the wood panelling in the campus hall, the exuberant yellow in a fresh lemon before it is sliced for tea. Smells, too, are stronger now, the rose bush on the pathway leading to the campus, the coffee shop she passes every morning on her way to work. Most people never find out how good it feels to feed off yourself. There's a concentrated strength at the source.

With Maria, Darya knows who she is, a solid visible thing, a proud woman made of muscle and bone, skin and breath. Each morning after their workout, they stop at the full-length mirror in the privacy nook at the exit. Before leaving the locker room, they openly scan one another, head-to-toe, slowly attending.

"You know, Darya," says Maria. "Those hips are definitely getting firmer. The bulge, it's almost gone."

Maria loves how Darya's milestones feel like they're hers. Their bodies are reshaping in similar ways as if they are cut from the same cloth. It is beautiful.

The day Darya stands on the scale and reaches her goal, they're four months into their plan. Sweet mother, you've done it, thinks Maria. Your face, it glows. And your body, it's been reshaped as something new. Darya, my dear, you've let go of forty pounds. You've lost six dress sizes. There's a waist now and a back swoop. You look taller.

They share a private world other women will never know. Sometimes, when Maria thinks about it, she feels sad. The blindness of thinking everything comes from outside yourself. That thought turns grown women into children, running from their problems, hiding from their very selves, acting like love-sick fools, kissing people who no longer love them.

Maria and Darya are walking back to work after lunch when they run into Jules, Darya's boss. A sheer blouse with a floppy bow at the neck, oversized man pants, and a stack of files in her arms, Jules is not a woman who stops anywhere long.

Off to the side of the hallway, with mobs of students passing and the unintelligible drone of too many voices and the smell of bodies, they engage in a rushed conversation, if it can be called that.

Jules says, "Love your new style." She's looking right at Darya as if she knows her. "Been meaning to ask. What'd you do? Hire an image consultant?" It's more than a little weird how Jules doesn't wait for an answer, as if she'd been accumulating a mouthful of comments and needed to purge. "Cute belt," she adds. "Makes your waist look smaller. And great lines on that suit. Where do you find clothes that fit so well?"

A few days later, Darya and Maria are lifting weights, each perched on their own bench, surrounded by mirrored walls. In the shiny silver, Darya notices Maria's arms, the ever so slight sagging on her bicep, the lack of rise in her bulge. She's surprised to see the woman she admires has an area of weakness. Her own muscle definition is much better, she's embarrassed to admit.

When they pause between sets, Darya curls her fingers around Maria's upper arms. She meets her eyes, hoping to show the compassion she feels. They all have ways in which they might improve. "Looking less strong," she says gently. "Better do more curls."

She only says it to be helpful. It's not meant as a criticism. They build each other up, push one another towards better versions of themselves. All of it is done in friendship. Maria has been measuring Darya for months, telling her what to do, acting like her boss or her mother. But when Darya makes this comment, Maria has a fit. Well, la-dee-da, aren't you the important one?

She slaps Darya's hand, backs away, and stomps out of the fitness centre, leaving Darya to finish alone. There was a time when this would've caused Darya to chase after her friend and apologize. Thank God, she's stronger now.

Darya refuses to let Maria make her think less of herself. She does twenty extra reps on her own, proving to anyone watching that she has real muscle now. She's started to wonder if maybe Maria resents her success. The way Maria refused to acknowledge her accomplishments in her job, how Darya's been getting attention for her looks. Nobody asks Maria where she gets her clothes.

It's an old school-girl ploy, running away to prove how valuable you are, hoping to be chased. Seems like maybe Maria is trying to control her. She liked Darya well enough when she was fat.

Maria is wondering if maybe it's time to set Darya loose. They aren't really working together anymore. A less needy person would've taken the hint when Maria cleared her stuff out of the staff locker room and started using the student facilities instead because at least they have change stalls.

She never asks Darya to join her, and yet Darya does. The

way that woman has been following her around for months, anybody would think they're roped together by the ankles. It felt good in the beginning to share goals, and together they accomplished great things. Problem is, they've lost all sense of privacy, all sense of boundaries.

Since Maria's wife took off with her younger lover, no one sees Maria naked, and she likes it that way. The day things go wrong in the change stall in the student locker room, Maria has no idea Darya is watching. Until the neck of her sweatshirt clears her chin and she threads her arms into the sleeves, pulling the shirt over her torso, she doesn't know Darya is in the stall.

Sweat makes her skin itch, so Maria no longer wears a bra. She's never had much in the way of breasts, and it makes her want to die to think Darya has seen what is missing. Yet, in a way, it almost seems fitting. After all the months of sharing secrets, maybe they are meant to finally encounter each other without pretense. If she's honest, Maria has to admit how much she wants to be recognized for her valiant effort.

Of all people, she expects Darya to understand. But when Maria bares all she dreams of becoming, she is found lacking. And the person standing over her with narrowed eyes and a still mouth is not some nosey staff member who doesn't understand. It is the woman she thought was her true friend.

She can no longer stomach this sort of betrayal. She feels like throwing up. Her lungs seem to have collapsed inside her rib cage. There's no air in the tiny stall. She's shocked when she manages to produce a sound from her lips. "Why are you here?" she demands, shaking. "Leave."

Darya never meant to watch. She's not unaware of the need to hold certain matters private. Heaven knows, she dislikes being watched herself. She's no longer seeing either man. She doesn't like how they look at her, would rather keep company with herself. But she's finally been promoted to senior instructor. About time those jerks took notice of her work. The study will be published in six months, maybe sooner.

When she interrupted Maria dressing, she'd had a thought she'd wanted to share. She'd read about intervals and how a person needs to blend longer ones with shorter ones, something new every day or the body grows accustomed and stops changing to meet the demands. She'd expected Maria to be as excited as she was about finding a new way to heighten their workouts.

The student change room smells of chlorine and shampoo with traces of female body secretions. Strands of hair float about in clumps. Nail clippings stick to the soles of running shoes. But she agrees with Maria, it is better with some privacy. At least there are change stalls and curtains here.

When she steps into the stall, Maria's face is covered. It's not Darya's fault that she gets an open view of the sharp ribs and hip bones, the puff of girlish breasts, the sucked-back hollow where other people carry a belly.

She'd been telling herself what they did together was brave. Without question, they have more courage than most, and people don't like women who can control themselves around food. It breeds dangerous levels of envy. It can start rumours.

A few days before the incident, Darya had bought new

clothes. They hadn't had a chance to look them over together. She was never really sure of what worked until she got an opinion from Maria. At the store, she'd tried on the last size that had fit her, and the pants slid off her butt. She'd wished Maria had been with her. They'd have enjoyed a good giggle. So here's what has happened—she's double-zero now. Until she'd achieved it, she hadn't even known there was such a thing. Some stores call the size double-extra-small.

Darya would be the first to admit what looks good clothed does not always look good naked. Bottoms are lumpy things without the swirl and swoosh of a skirt. A pair of pants only fit right if the skin between the hip bones forms a shallow basin.

Yet, something is wrong, she can feel it. When she backs out of Maria's stall, she is unable to look away and unable to stay, feeling bad for not helping her friend.

If the timing had been different, she might have talked to Maria right then, cleared things up between them, except a new position has opened up for an academic coordinator, and she really wants an interview. She needs to focus on herself now. Once the job is hers, maybe things will be different. She tells Maria they can't work out together until the interview is over, and she begins to do her exercising at a gym closer to home.

After Darya leaves, Maria's bottom lands hard on the cold bench in her change stall. There is someone in the next stall. She heard footsteps and rustling and the unzipping of an exercise bag. Why couldn't they choose a stall that is not next to another person's?

And Darya should never have pushed herself into the private space. Friends do not do such things. Shaking, Maria finishes dressing, putting on her bottoms, lifting her bum to fit the velvety warmth of her sweatpants over her hips. Below the elastic waist, the gathered fabric billows.

When she draws back the curtain and steps into the empty locker room, no one is watching. The person in the next stall has finished their business. The corner of the bench rams Maria's knee as she hurries past, but it does nothing to slow her down. Although she is limping, she goes onward to the exercise room and claims the same bike she was riding the day she met Darya.

She'd been drawn to Darya's red-faced enthusiasm, the way she slammed down on the pedals, her open warmth. It felt good to get some attention. Back then, she was still with Sammy.

But after Darya catches her naked, they drift apart like Darya is avoiding her. The next day, Darya tells Maria she'll be too busy with her career to exercise together, and she'll have to save lunch hours for studying. They never work out together again. And later, when Maria thinks it through, she'll decide that Darya found a new place to workout, maybe a new exercise buddy.

But Maria goes through the motions on her own now, working out every day, eating with care. She begins to use the change stall farthest from the exit and to keep an open ear. If she hears footsteps, she covers herself. Part of her expects Darya to return, apologetic and needful.

She imagines turning her away, pushing her out of the

change stall, telling her to mind her own life. And then she imagines the opposite version, forgetting what happened and welcoming Darya near because who else will ever understand?

Darya is not there when things fall apart. She keeps meaning to check on Maria, but at first, she enjoys exercising closer to home. Then Ms. Wonderful steals the promotion, and Darya is disgusted with herself. She doesn't want to tell Maria. As months begin to pass, everything starts to seem pointless. Darya is plagued by nausea, dizziness and headaches. When she goes home for the once-a-month Sunday dinner at her mom's, things get weird. Sitting in the oversized dining room with a lace tablecloth under plastic, Darya is mindful to eat an acceptable amount, but her mother keeps nagging her to go see a doctor. She's worried her daughter has undiagnosed cancer.

Rumours reach Darya before she is given the full story. *My God, did you hear what happened to that woman? They say she had to be removed by ambulance. . . . I could never be anorexic. I like eating. . . . I find super skinny unattractive, don't you? . . . To tell the truth, I always thought there was something wrong with her.*

Darya is grateful when Maria's boss comes to her office and fills her in. There is such depth of concern on Grace's face, Darya worries that Grace might burst into tears. All of this hints at an understanding that does not quite make sense. Not to be rude, but Grace is fat.

Turns out, she'd been bringing Maria food. The morning everything happened, Grace gave Maria a small container of lemon yogurt. Later in the hospital, Maria tells Darya she really did try to take care of things. She'd been given a serious talking to only the day before. Grace had told her if there wasn't a significant change, she would have to involve human resources.

The thick cream made Maria gag, but she intended to swallow every mouthful. No, she did not want to lose her job. She'd already lost her wife and her home. But the yogurt container slipped from her hand and dropped to the floor. If she hurried, she could mop up what spilled and eat the rest before anyone knew.

She rolled back her chair, stood up, and folded at the waist. Everything was okay until she reached forward, and a dull pain crushed her lower back, making it impossible for her to straighten up. She collapsed to the floor, moaning. Spilt yogurt in her hair, her body was determined to humiliate her. Warm liquid trickled down her legs.

In the industrial green room with a forcefully cheerful painting of ducks splashing about in a pond, Maria keeps her personal items on an over-bed table. She has an MP3 player and earbuds, a romance novel, and a wide-toothed comb, plus ultra-soft tissues and lanolin hand cream. The place smells like old soup from the can, mushroom probably, and people dying.

On doctor's orders, she accepts the feeding tube they shove up her nose and down her throat. Although she wants to rip it out, for weeks she wears the tube all the time, a slow drip to her stomach beyond her control. The tube is taped to her nose, tucked behind her ear, and attached to a refeeding bag. She is marked for what she's become, and she cannot tell another living soul who she was.

So many people do not understand, she starts wondering what's real. She swallows whatever hideous food they put on the ugly brown plastic tray. And she fakes disclosure during group therapy. It's not hard, just listen to other people's tales of woe and steal bits and pieces for your own. She takes bed rest and does physio for her spine with a fraction of her innate intensity.

When Darya shows up at her bedside the same day she's admitted, her face melts in a puddle of snot and tears. She can't stop shaking her head. No, no, no. She tells Darya the whole sordid mess, every detail including peeing herself, and she feels a little better. They do not need to talk about the change stall or the months apart.

Darya visits faithfully every day after work. She brings deep-fried chicken, greasy pepperoni pizza, fries soaked in gravy, stuff she knows better than to be putting in her mouth. Even with a tube pricking her nostril and pain in her back, Maria sees the truth. Darya is getting fat.

Before Maria went into the hospital, Darya had already stopped going to the gym. She no longer tastes her food and she avoids mirrors. None of it means anything without Maria. The sight of her once powerful friend helpless as a newborn, being force-fed by a tube, unable to walk more than five minutes. Darya sees what she has to do.

She fights the nurses until they allow her to eat in Maria's room. People are so judgmental. Those nurses look at Darya's waist, the size two pants she now wears, and they form conclusions. But then, Darya dares the nurses to watch them eating in Maria's room. None of it is easy, swallowing that slime, knowing where the fat will place itself on her body, the greasy chicken, the congealed gravy, the chemically enriched pepperoni on the pizza.

Once a person tastes the concentrated strength at the source, nothing else satisfies. Maria's back mends, and she puts on a few pounds. They remove the feeding tube and let her nourish herself. Her cheeks pinken. A fierce flame returns to Maria's eyes, but she only allows Darya to see it.

In the container she keeps in her purse, Darya starts bringing the right kind of food. After a while, the nurses no longer watch. It is possible once again for the friends to share truth.

Darya peels back the plastic top, glances over her shoulder to make sure they're alone and offers Maria a helping. They drop a glassy slice of cucumber onto their tongues at the exact same time. The taste comes from within.

The Love Drug

My son and I sat side-by-side on big square chairs, both of us rigid with stress, looking through the tall windows to the world outside. Rehab was located an hour from Welltown, tucked into the foothills in a modernist building with angled roofs and wide views. On a clear day, brave mountains rise above the golden rolls of hay. Deer were known to visit, coyotes too, with hawks swooping down the sunset sky for a kill.

"What the hell, Mom? You told me you were okay." The visiting room was filled with loved ones gripping armrests.

Kyle covered the back of my unsteady hand with his, and I settled a little. It was well into week one of my stay. Over the worst of the physical stuff, I was dealing with the emotional chaos. Kyle had begun to unravel the truth.

"I'm sorry," I said. The words clogged my throat. And what with the panic escalating inside of me, I would have liked to have taken a big good gulp of fresh oxygen. But seeing me gasp, that would've only made it harder for Kyle to believe my apology.

"How am I supposed to trust you when all you do is lie?" His lips thinned into a small straight line.

"You were busy with school." Even I knew that was nonsense. "I didn't want to burden you," I added, unable to stop trying. He yanked his hand away, and I felt like the worse mother alive.

"That's not fair," he said. "When have I ever not been there for you?'

A year earlier, when his dad decided to go for more than the occasional sleepover and live full-time with his mistress, Kyle had offered to move back home with me. He'd been working on his business degree and had settled into a bachelor apartment near campus.

I'd told him, "Nothing doing. I am a grown woman, and I'll take care of myself." Fine job I did of that. He was the one I'd called from the emergency ward. He'd delivered me to detox in his beat-up Honda. A few days later, he'd taxied me to rehab.

Before I'd overdosed, the drug was doing its job better than usual. I'd slipped into the void, was covered in stardust. And then, oops—I'd vanished into thin air. No longer breathing, loss of consciousness, sweet yes. It'd have been better for everyone if I'd stayed gone.

But no, I'd dragged Kyle into my messed-up business. There I was, sunk into the shiny white floor in the emergency ward of the local hospital, sickened to death with myself. All my regrets seemed to drop into my sensible brown leather shoes, the truth of what I'd become. Forced to sit in the uncomfortable stackable chair against the cold wall in a busy corridor, I could not look up. I wanted to crawl inside myself and die. A nurse with better things to be doing walked by every ten minutes or so to make sure I was still conscious.

Kyle had arrived like a saint with his head glowing white. He deserved a mother, not the loser he'd found sitting alone in that corridor, that sad woman with stringy blond hair damp with sweat and tangled in knots where she'd spun strands around her dried-out index finger way too many times.

I'd purged my list of sins to the sweet boy. I mean, seriously. What kind of mother does that? It should've been enough that he came to the hospital. I should've played it down, created a diversion, lied.

Instead, I made everything worse. The hideous things I'd done. Saying my cell phone was broken when I'd been too high to take his calls. Pretending I had the flu when I'd missed his birthday. It had been selfish. My need to clear the slate was only a transference of pain. He'd have been better off not knowing.

Truth is better served to those whose mouth is already familiar with the taste of lies. People like me, who've fallen from grace, not those who are faithful and kind. Kyle visited me every day in rehab. For his sake, I had to keep trying. But I needed a person my own age, someone who understood, better yet, a person in no position to judge.

And then, in walked Lalita. It was the second week of my

stay at the fun-house freak show when she floated into the meeting room dressed all in black with her gossamer grey scarf twinkling white light. We were doing our daily group session. Lost causes, all of us, we stared at this creature who wore a spiral galaxy over her sharp shoulders. I doubt there was a single person in the room not taken by the woman with a head of close-cropped silver hair.

I'd been worrying my cuticles raw, disgusted with how I did not fit in even at rehab, the last resort for hopeless people.

Lalita scanned the adoring faces in the circle and stopped at mine. She pointed to the space between my chair and the one next to me, a gap not big enough for any person.

She was late; not by a few minutes, but by half an hour. Under normal circumstances, that would've been a punishable offence; the guilty party subjected to a lecture on the fundamentals of respect. But the whole circle shifted to make an opening for Lalita. We lifted our chairs under our butts and did a half-bent shuffle to make room for her. The blue-eyed boy with a Love Hurts tattoo on his shaved head fetched Lalita a chair and slid it into place right next to mine.

"This is me," said Lalita, sitting down.

My heart was aswirl, twirling around like a crazed idiot. Even when I was full-out sober, not a sprinkle of stardust on me, some moments intoxicated.

"Déjà vu, damn it," she said with a snort, rewrapping her scarf. "Can't say I am happy to be here. But hey, I'm Lalita."

We went around the circle, giving our names. "Hanna here," I said. "Ecstasy," I added as a bonus, and she grinned.

Benzos were Lalita's problem. It started with a prescription to help her manage the panic attacks that showed up unannounced at embarrassing moments. Unlike me, she'd been able to tell us a lot about herself right from the start. She had children and grandchildren and a high-powered job in upper-end real estate and more than her fair share of stories.

Like the time she'd greeted home buyers in classic Madonna style, wearing only a bra on her upper half. She'd put on slacks but had been too out of it to finish dressing. The young couple she'd toured through the property never said anything about her appearance, although the wife was fidgety and the husband a bit too eager.

"Good thing I happened to be wearing my hot black lace bra," she'd said, her teeth showing as she laughed.

The group howled. I mean, people were tearing up with laughter. I wasn't sure it was really appropriate given the circumstances, but even Grant, the facilitator, could not stop himself.

I was heading back to my cell, the tiny room with a single bed and a minuscule dresser and barely enough room to move, when Lalita caught me in the hall. I'd been shuffling over the plush carpet alone, wondering where everyone went after the meeting, how they disappeared so quickly? A guy in a blue cleaning uniform was vacuuming. We waited for him to move to the side before continuing.

Tugging my arm, Lalita brought me closer. "Thank God, you're here," she said. "These kids know nothing. If they mess up, they have the rest of their lives to get clean and start over. But you and me, our lives are locked in place . . . houses, kids and careers we can't leave."

We walked arm-in-arm, me and this stunningly beautiful woman who also understood what it means to have regrets. As our friendly on-site therapist liked to point out, the only times I'd been comfortable in social situations was when I was under the influence. I'd not exactly done well with relationships. Lalita's son lived in Europe, and her daughter refused to speak to her.

"Those morons who call themselves doctors, they should've warned me. I should sue their asses good and hard."

"Yeah, same here," I said. Doctors had nothing to do with my problems, but I nodded along like a bobblehead. And why? Because I appreciated company, a person at my side waiting for my reactions and caring what I said.

Lalita claimed her problem was a medical condition brought on by incompetent doctors. For sure, they should've been more careful. I agreed with that. But how she openly judged others in group, it made me uncomfortable. The way she whispered false sympathy for the shy guy with the shaved head and fentanyl problem. By his own admission, he'd done bad things for his drug. His family had forsaken him. Before rehab, he was living under a park bench. Lalita put herself above the rest of us. I knew it, disliked it, and was drawn to it all at once.

She was ignoring certain facts, such as how she'd needed two weeks to detox while I'd only needed two days. Plus, she'd falsified prescriptions and ordered pills off the dark web, same as the rest of us. There were no doctors involved in that. Denial was the first challenge any of us faced.

Under a disco ball spinning purple and green stars, I'd seen stuff others would never dream of, mouths opening wide to pleasure, groups of men hugging, women running their fingers over each other's lips. The love drug promised compassion and kindness on a viral level, plenty for everyone.

Was it a menopausal awakening of a uniquely stupid kind or simply soul-crushing loneliness? Night after night, I'd sat alone in our heritage home on the Prairie Heights hill, torturing myself with old movies featuring men who loved their pretty wives, eating popcorn and contemplating different ways I might kill myself.

At supper, Lalita joined me once again. The dining area had round tables, white tablecloths and comfy chairs, plus a help-yourself counter where residents got themselves something to eat.

"How's the food?" she asked. "Tasteless as ever?"

We were lined up at the counter side-by-side, filling our plates. I glanced at the potato salad, the chicken breast, the shrunken peas. None of it looked like something you should put in your mouth.

The whole time I was in rehab, I never learned to enjoy the shared eating experience. Who wanted to listen to the grinding of worn teeth or see the saliva awash in a sad mouth? Nobody in their right mind wanted to sit down at the table to wide-spread alienation.

I had more than my fill of awkward company outside of meals. The one time my manager had dared to visit, she'd toned down her normally perky voice and tried to pretend she wasn't mortified. My union job as a library tech at the college gave me excellent coverage, she'd wanted to assure me.

Most moments in life, even the brutal ones, have a redeeming component, an experience undeniably good no matter how brief. The counsellors kept telling us to seek those moments with gag-me-please true-life stories.

"I was sitting on a park bench alone," offered Robert. He liked to talk in group. "First day sober, and a robin started pecking the lawn in front of me . . ."

And our girl Charlene, she said, "The lady at the grocery store checkout . . ." Charlene was clenching her hands. She'd been with us only two days when she shared her feel-good story. "That woman smiled at me and asked how I was. Not much to most people, but nobody had spoken to me for days. I was trying to get clean. I dunno, she helped me."

With dinners at rehab, the one redeeming experience was golden topped, airy as clouds and chewy. I'd hardly put anything on my plate, a scoop of peas, a sad-looking hunk of chicken, when I noticed the warm buns nested in a linen napkin in a big wooden bowl. My mouth watered at the possibilities.

"Have one," I said to Lalita, nudging the bowl closer to her. "They're actually good."

Lifting the napkin with red polished nails, Lalita leaned in for a whiff, and pleasure flooded her angular face. She plucked a warm bun from the bowl, delicately ripped off a piece, and instead of eating it herself, offered it to me.

I took the bread in my mouth. Right there, with people waiting, I let the soft dough melt over my tongue and turn chewy in my own juices. Ask any hungry person what gratitude is. Endless talking, promises of better days, setting mini-goals like staying clean for the next half-hour, learning to divert what they politely called suicidal ideation. Like blowing smoke rings from a hookah. What did any of that mean when you had warm bread in your mouth?

After that, I couldn't get enough of Lalita. We sat together at a plastic table, and I wolfed down my food. Yep, I hung on her every word, followed her about, and sat with her in group and for meals.

We had plunked ourselves down in front of the washing machines. It was three weeks into my stay, only one week into Lalita's, but that's how desperate we were for entertainment. We were mesmerized by the swirls of colours and our clothes rolling in soapy water.

Lalita had been sharing since we'd met, lots of stuff about the funny things she did when high, complaints about her partner and kids, rants about doctors. She didn't talk about why she'd started using until that afternoon sitting in front of our soapy clothes swashing around in hot water.

She'd thought it was her heart the first time she experienced a panic attack—the crushed chest, the tight throat, the sickening dread. She'd been halfway through showing a sandstone mansion on the Arrow River when she collapsed on the kitchen floor made of fine handcrafted faint blue marble. She'd cried out in pain, grabbing her clenched heart, trying to breathe.

Moments earlier, she'd been opening the dual convection ovens and showing off the gas grill. From the floor, she'd called out to the fancy guy viewing the house, "Pull out your damn cell phone. Call 9–1–1."

She hadn't been in the emergency ward half an hour when they'd told her there was nothing wrong with her. "Nothing wrong doesn't feel like dying, dammit," she'd snarled. They'd given her four benzos to take at a rate of one a day and a word of caution. She'd promised to go see a doctor right away, something she never did.

If you swallowed enough feelings, they swelled inside you, an overriding sense of futility, thoughts that wanted you gone. Even my husband could not love me. Old and alone, I saw it as a situation unlikely to improve. I'd taken to wandering late at night, first in the neighbourhood, then in the bright lights of downtown, past people sleeping in alcoves, and prostitutes and partiers heading into nightclubs.

I'd hear the noise whenever a front door to a club swung open. The relentless grind of disco gave me an abiding sense of hope. Maybe it was how unstoppable it seemed. Maybe it was the volume. People always came out of those buildings laughing, arm-in-arm, giddy with abandon. I'd been decent on the dance floor as a younger person.

When a woman in red leather and another in a pink tutu joined a third woman wearing a black suit clearly meant for a man, I wanted to be part of their group. As they stepped through the doors to the Infinitesimal Joy nightclub, I followed. Earlier that evening, I'd stood on the High Bridge, pressed against the metal railing, looking down at the dark river. In comparison, the risks seemed minor.

When a young man with a shaved head and a clean-cut suit offered me a sly wink and said, "Wantee? Wantee? It's pretty good." Well, I nodded yes, because why not? He put two heart-stamped pink pills in my hand and kissed me on the cheek like I was his favourite aunt. I could've melted, that's how badly I needed affection. "You look like you could really use some," he'd added.

Caught in the pounding heaves of flesh, the bobbing heads, the thumping churn of incessant guttural phrases, and the deadly undertow of electronic bass and a drum machine, I struggled to keep my mouth above water. For a while, I felt more out of place than ever, cowering inside. I wondered, should I try to find the bald guy? Ask for another pill? Then it happened.

Addicts were warned about avoiding triggers—such as stories about being elevated—for good reasons. Lalita relished every word I gave her, those thin fingers on her neckline, those lips of hers wet.

People who've never been high can't imagine. Colours buzzed, sounds sizzled on my tongue, I felt the touch of life in every vital organ, my heart did calypso, my brain pirouetted. My skin was so tender the air could bruise me. Because let's be honest, until then, I'd never been awake, even during the most important moments in my life. The birth of my son. My mother's death from lung cancer.

With purple and green stars dancing all around me, I raised

my hand to examine this tool I'd long neglected, wondering at what it was capable of doing. The smoosh of my thumb where it pressed my finger filled me with mother's love, all warm and gushy. There's no better way to describe it. I let my hand open. Air rushed between my fingers. I walked forward and joined with the nearest person I could touch.

As we walked the circular path around the facility, Kyle pushed ahead as if he might escape. I'd been in rehab for three weeks. Seemed to me I should be the one wanting escape, but his lean frame remained two steps ahead of mine. The path was the geographical boundary of my confinement, a fact he pretended not to know.

The birds were better company. Hardy black-capped chickadees in fluffed-up grey suits, perched in spruce trees, sang their cheeky songs. And bad-ass crows, high above on dead branches, cawing proudly upon our foolishness.

Soon they would set me loose. I'd have to go back to my job in the library and the big empty house, the very life I'd tried to obliterate.

On our third trip around the facility, Kyle waved towards a bench, a shy smile on his thin face. Honestly, this was the first sign during our so-called visit that he might actually want to be together with me.

I joined him on the wooden bench. Noticing too late that it was covered in dew, I felt the wet spot forming on the bum of my pants.

From his pocket, Kyle pulled out a piece of paper folded

into a tiny square, like a love letter written by a schoolboy. "I printed this for you," he said, placing the note on my lap.

I unfolded the paper, remembering a better moment . . . the crayon drawing he'd given me when he was four, how he'd proudly waited for me to take the crinkled piece of paper from his little hands. He'd drawn three stick people with wavy arms and V-shaped legs standing in front of a gargantuan orange sun. He had a parent on either side, his mother and father each holding one of his hands. Things were different now.

On the bench, under a gloomy sky, his mouth grew small and tight as he waited impatiently for me to read the note. It took me a minute or two to catch my breath.

I smoothed out the paper, as if that made any difference, and handed it back to him. "Kyle, have you ever once known your mother to belong to a club? I appreciate the effort. It's just not my thing."

That brought Kyle to his feet. He made a big show of crushing the paper into a ball and tossing it into the nearby trash can. I was thinking that would be sufficient, that he wouldn't need to say anything more. He'd punish me with a little pout, and we'd be good. But the boy he used to be was no longer with us.

A man now, he stood over me, a fool of a woman squat upon the bench with a wet spot on her pants. He was large and loud. "Excuse me for thinking you might want to keep busy, take your mind off your problems, maybe get out to the mountains."

I couldn't decide if I wanted to apologize or tell him to leave me the hell alone. We would've both felt better if he'd come right out and said what he meant. He wanted to keep me busy, as if that was all I needed to stay sober—a hobby. Learn to paint, dance the rhumba, romp up steep mountains with strangers. You betcha. That was just what I needed.

We sat through family therapy every week. We were supposed to be learning how to be honest with each other. They didn't take into account the consequences of truth, how it twisted love into obligation and turned mothers into guilty children.

The first time Kyle asked if I had a drug problem, I'd almost confessed. Hugging my knees, my feet on the seat of my favourite blue velvet chair, I'd rocked back and forth. Maybe I could've told him, it might've felt better, but at what cost? Let's be honest. There was only so much a person could lose before they ceased to exist.

It'd been months since Gunter left. I'd been putting up a decent front, or so I told myself, but a friend of Kyle's had spread the rumour. Young people went to the nightclub, people who knew my son. I should've been smarter.

Until then, we'd never had to work at being honest with each other. I could look my boy in the eye, ask a question, and know his answer was truthful. Something broke the day I left him guessing whether his gut feelings were a thing he could rely on.

He sat perfectly still, waiting. "What's going on, Mom? Talk to me."

"Okay, fine. I went to that nightclub. But only because I was lonely. It's awful living in this big empty house. When a co-worker invited me for a night out, I went. But I didn't stay. The music was too loud, and I sure as heck did not do drugs.

That's a ridiculous idea, especially at my age," I huffed good and loud in his face.

We both knew he did not believe me, yet I could not stop the charade, and he could not openly accuse his mother of lying. In the acid burn of silence, I told myself I no longer needed those pills, I could stop any time. And once I had, there'd be no reason to hurt him.

I drew him into a fierce hug, pushing his ribs into mine. He went rag doll, like he'd left his own body. "Why anyone would say such a thing, I do not know," I said, trying to squeeze him back to life. "Be careful who you believe."

Lalita told me when she was in withdrawal, the dimmer switch on her nervous system got turned almost to black. Every time she was on the downward swing, she got a sinus pain like her brain had been frozen and was starting to thaw. And she'd get these creepy inner vibrations, more intense than trembling and louder too, a buzzing inside like a hive of bees nesting in her chest. She'd have a short temper, get into a wrestling match with strangers in line for their cappuccinos, find herself banned from her favourite coffee shop.

Rehab was not much different. In here, if you got caught using, they kicked you out. I'd seen it happen. They tested the purity of our intentions any time they felt like it. On a regular basis, they'd herd us into the nearest washroom, stand there with a clear view of our soon-to-be-naked asses, hand us each an individually wrapped cleansing wipe, and command us to void ourselves.

We were in Lalita's room when the counsellors arrived. We

hadn't been using anything except friendship, if that's a drug. Okay, honest. The way she'd held her chest when she talked about bees, I'd almost believed she was experiencing a pain not so different from mine. For a moment, I felt less alone.

They'd sent females, one for Lalita and one for me, a false nod to a dignity that was not possible. This wasn't the first time they'd made me void, and it didn't get easier. Afterwards, my skin prickled, and my knees were mush. Decent people did not have to prove their honesty. The hideous things I'd done replayed in my mind. Taking drugs with coffee at my desk. Showing up for my niece's wedding completely outside myself. Eating spaghetti the first time I met Kyle's girlfriend, sitting opposite her at that nice Italian restaurant, worried out of my mind that I might slop food . . . because, to be perfectly honest, I was not precisely sure where to find my own mouth.

The test was done, but there was no proof of my recovery. An addict could not be redeemed no matter what the counsellors would have us believe. The past is forever. No one really forgets. I wanted to choke myself, be gone, not have to continue with the detestable business of being me. When one cuticle bled, I tore at a new one. The free edges of my nails, the white part normal people have, were all gone. There was nothing left but the ragged edges over the angry red skin that should have been protected.

Sitting on the edge of Lalita's bed after the test-takers had left us alone, I expected her to offer me comfort. She'd told me her secrets. In lots of ways, she'd done worse. Yet she was unmoved by my clearly unmanageable anxiety. All I warranted from her was a quick awkward glance before she turned her back and walked away. Moments later, she returned with a box of tissues, although I had not shed a single tear. At least I had that dignity. She set the box on the bed next to me, then she grabbed her gossamer scarf that twinkled white light, and she floated away.

The next morning, three days from my release, I stopped by Lalita's room, and she was already gone. I seemed to always be trying to catch up, competing for Lalita's precious time. She claimed to be free of spirit. She did not care for making plans. When I arrived at our breakfast table, all the seats were taken.

I stood at her table, wondering what to do, waiting like an idiot for her to look up and welcome me in. It was a known character flaw with me, believing people were my friends when they were not. I had a habit of trusting the untrustworthy, of getting tossed aside. Lalita sparkled for everyone else but pretended not to see me.

After the first time I'd used, the empathy I'd awakened never returned. A three-hour virus at best, the kindness I'd swallowed was spent, never to be replenished. A person can only be heightened once. After that, it's a bad, paint-by-numbers piece of art, tedious in its predictability, ridiculous in its meticulously futile effort. I'd get properly thizzed out, enough to numb the hurt. But in the days that followed after getting high, I'd be worse than ever, emotionally bleeding to death. I'd vow to myself I would stop. Never again, I'd say, and I'd mean it.

Hours had passed since breakfast when Lalita found me in

my room reading a book. "Are you avoiding me?" she asked.

I hated being mocked, how she twisted the truth like that. "Uh, no," I said, pressing my hands on the open book in my lap. If only I'd told her then and there that she'd hurt me. Forever after, it haunted me knowing I'd allowed her to ignore me and then pretend I was the one being cold.

I was surprised when she chose to sit next to me later in group. The young man with a fentanyl problem was sharing, his chin quivering in a way that reminded me of Kyle. As he was talking, Lalita took my hand. She'd never done anything like that before.

A part of me wanted my hand back. Another part hoped she'd never let go.

I'd only done the drug in company for a few months because I began to witness myself flailing around—hours later when it was too late to change what I'd done. I'd wake the next morning with evidence tapes in my brain, ready to be played and rewound and played again. Me pulling my shirt over my head. Me showing the world my old-lady bra. Me laughing hysterically at the weird knot of my belly button stamped into the pillowy mound of stretch marks.

Maybe it should've never happened, or maybe I'd always been ready for the taking. Safe from watchful eyes, I started doing my drugs at home. I'd have two capsules after supper and dance in the darkened living room wearing flannel pyjamas with trance music I found on the radio turned up ear-achingly loud. At first, it'd been a Friday night reward for making it through the week. Then I added over-the-hump day, as I called Wednesday.

It became harder to hide the constant crying at work, the continuing excuses, the wanton avoidance of life. I'd pretended to have the flu, which worsened and became pneumonia. I'd lied myself into two months off work. After I'd returned, the only way I could make it through the day was to think about that next pill on my tongue.

Two days before my release, Kyle left me hanging. I sat in the boxy chair, gripping the armrest alone, while people talked to their loved ones. Lalita was far away in a corner with the guy she called her life partner. She was not a fan of marriage. It made her feel caged.

My son had left me staring into my own empty hands. Thanks to him, I had to endure gazes from all the other addicts who thought they were better than me because they had people who stayed at their side through thick and thin, fucked-up and clean, dead or alive. I thought about that, dead or alive . . . yeah, that was an item yet to be fully tested by the people in the room, although many had stood at the abyss, both confused and certain, so close to gone. I'd taken in their stories. I'd heard what they'd said.

My fingers twitched, and I stuck them one by one into my mouth, ripping my cuticles, lapping up my own blood. It was sick what I became when I felt abandoned.

Visiting hour was almost over when Kyle waltzed in like nothing was the matter, his overloaded backpack slipping off his shoulders. "Had to talk to my prof about the final project." He dropped into the empty chair that had been waiting for him for fifty-five useless minutes. "Group project is a gong show. Half the team didn't show up. The rest of us did all the work. Great system for them, I guess."

"Where were you?"

Kyle's hand stopped mid-reach for his water bottle. "I just said! I had to speak to my prof. Three more weeks of classes and then finals. I'll be glad when it's all over."

"I've been sitting here alone with people staring at me for an hour. You could've called." My voice was all hushed like it was some kind of secret.

He looked at his watch, his lips a small knot on that long face, his jaw sharp.

"Do you have any idea what it's like being stuck in this place? I look forward to your visits all day."

Jackson, that creep of a guy I'd never liked, was sitting in the cluster of chairs beside us. His whole damn family was visiting, a wife and three teenagers, no less. None of them looked angry or upset.

Kyle crossed his arms over his chest. His foot tapped the floor.

"You couldn't see the prof some other time? You couldn't tell him you have a mother who is sick and needs your visit?"

"Okay, enough." Kyle rose from his chair, reaching for his backpack. He cared not how loud he was. Every person in the room rubber-necked towards us. Like I wasn't hurting enough. "I do my best for you, Mom. There are things in my life besides your addiction."

By the time I rose from my chair, he was at the door. I chased him, grabbed his arm. He turned to face me.

"Sorry for putting you out," I said. Not the slightest change on his puckered-up sourpuss face. "Don't come if it's such a hardship."

Then I turned on my heels and marched away, expecting him to chase after me, yearning for him to claim me, dying inside when he let me go.

They told us to concentrate on the basics. Do yoga and walk. Eat lots of vegetables and get plenty of rest. Even when we couldn't sleep, if we lay still, our bodies would heal. That was what they told us. They underestimated the persistence of thoughts, of how, in the dark, a mind can feast upon itself, and a body can manifest pain.

After Kyle's visit, I did what I always did when I couldn't sleep: I hauled myself out of the sweaty bed and took a jittery walk down the dim halls. I'd found it was the only cure. Other evenings, Lalita had been at my side. We would go back and forth, our bare feet on the carpet, our voices freed by the silence around us. I wondered if she remembered all the things she'd confessed to me. Revealing private feelings was practically a compulsion with her. She seemed oblivious to how it incriminated her. Being unfaithful, disappearing for weeks, a wildcat temper. I was amazed her partner stuck around.

When Kyle had first noticed changes in me, I'd claimed it was a virus. When the virus persisted, he'd figured it was depression—not a completely inaccurate diagnosis. He'd stop by after university and find me hollowed out and wasted, depleted of goodness. He'd bring me homemade soup and smoked salmon and tell me to take omega-3.

I was deep in memories, lingering over all the bad things I did as a mother, when I spotted Lalita wandering the hall like me, her black robe drifting, her tall, confident frame filling the empty spaces around her. I made a point of not hurrying, of keeping a safe distance. If she hadn't stopped at her door, we probably wouldn't have spoken.

"Hey," I said.

"Yeah."

We stood looking furtively at each other, it was two in the bloody morning, and suddenly we were strangers with nothing to say. She rubbed the brush of silver hair on her delicate head, her default habit for self-soothing. I'd seen it before, but I hadn't seen the skin on her forearm. She practically always wore long-sleeved tops, even under her bathrobe. Alone in the hall, perhaps because she did not expect to see anyone, her arms were not covered. When she lifted her hand to her head, the sleeve of her gown slid downwards, revealing bare skin. The underside of her forearm was marked with scars, deep lines of clean cuts healed white, a red scab where a fresh cut had recently been made.

She caught my eyes and tugged down the sleeve, turning around and retreating to her room, shutting the door behind her.

The final day before my release, Lalita and I played our game one last time. She'd been collecting new admirers every day.

There'd been no possibility of sitting with her for breakfast, and there'd certainly been no point standing by the table, waiting to be seen.

I had other things on my mind. Kyle had not been to see me since our quarrel, and he wasn't taking my calls. I'd given up texting. In spite of the complaining, rehab had been a safe zone. Soon I would be dumped back into the real world, and I wasn't sure I could cope. Maybe I'd be like Lalita, forced to make a return appearance. For sure, they'd be watching me at work, and I wouldn't get away with much.

Lalita was on her yoga mat in the big room with windows and a hardwood floor. When I tried to set my mat down next to hers, so did another woman. With bold red hair that reached all the way to her waist, she was clearly a better match for a person of Lalita's charms. Yet, I did not back down. Maybe if I hadn't been so beggared for attention, empty bowl in hand, driven mad by the hunger. There was only so long a person could go without contact.

From the corner of my eye, I caught a light rising up Lalita's face, igniting her eyes. She lifted her chin with a confidence impossible to ignore. With the wave of her arm, she nudged the other woman to the side. "Hanna was here first. Let her in."

We hadn't talked since I'd seen the cuts she made on her own flesh. I'd have liked to have told her the scars made me sad. Maybe I could've convinced her I'd guard her secret as my own. As she stretched her body into the poses, I understood. The hunger of it settled into the emptiness inside me. The certain knowledge we would never be close, and I would keep trying as long as the opportunity was within reach. I was not surprised when, after yoga, she gathered new companions and left me behind.

Sometimes it'd taken one day, other times two, but sooner or later, what went up always came down. Every part of my body would hurt. My jaw would feel broken. My teeth became raw nerve ends from the relentless grinding. As peaceful as the world became under the love drug, it was a war zone after, dead bodies everywhere.

The day of my final defeat, I'd bought from a greasy guy with a bald spot and dirty fingernails instead of waiting for a reliable source. You don't know what junk a person like that puts into the drugs they sell. I'd taken four capsules. In one swallow, I'd become a messed-up void with a liquified brain and lungs pleading for me to give up the ghost. I'd wobble-run to the nearest washroom, the whispers of co-workers at my back. I'd heard them outside my cubicle, along with the sounds of students and whoever was peeing and flushing in the nearby cubicles. The story ended when I crashed to the floor. Fade to black, as they say.

After the naloxone, they'd taken me to the emergency ward and sat me down in a chair to recover. I'd been wavery, dropped back into unconsciousness once. They'd had to give me a second dose, and so I needed monitoring. But I'd sensed how the nurse resented my presence. I was using time and resources others needed more. I agreed with her. I was a waste of space. Then Kyle came to the emergency ward.

I should've known I could trust my boy. On my last morning in rehab, he drove me home. He skipped classes to do it. I was packing my suitcase when he walked into my room. They'd already given me my last therapy session, a list of resources, and a booking for follow-up. When I tried to say bye to Lalita, she refused to open her door.

Kyle offered to stay with me a few nights. I told him, "No, I'm a grown woman. I'll take care of myself." It hurt to face him, and I never knew what to say anymore. In many ways, it was easier when he was mad at me. Since the first time I held him in the crook of my arm, his tiny head smeared with sandy blond hair, his clear eyes taking everything in, I haven't wanted to turn away. But the tilt of his chin, the way he looked up at me—it was a mistake. And I didn't know how to warn him.

We sat on the couch in my living room, a view of the city skyline outside the window. I forgot how much a person could see from my house. The white light of office towers glowed brighter than the setting sun. Thick fog layered over the river. I wondered if I should change my mind and ask him to stay, wondered if having him near would ease the weight over my chest, help me breathe.

He patted my knee, looking straight ahead at the slowly blackening sky beyond the high-rises. "Never forget I love you, Mom."

While I guarded the ugly truth inside my skull, the things I'd done, the things I might do, he repeated the words I most wanted to hear. Even when I held my open palms out to him, shaking my head, unable to speak, he refused to stop.

"I love you," he said again. "I'm here for you always, Mom."

I whispered in his ear during the long goodbye. My lips on his flesh, I wanted there to be nothing between us. "I love you too. I'm sorry." The words knocked around in my head. For a while, they were all I heard.

Crossing the Line

"Anyone can run a marathon," declared the wet-behind-the-ears creature in charge. Her blond-streaked brown hair was fastened in a messy bun, off-centre at the back of her head. For a finishing touch, she'd coiled a blue bandana around her forehead. "All it takes is one simple thing," she added like a tease.

"Showing up!" yelled the devotees in advanced-level running shoes with GPS wristwatches and water belts.

Here we go again, thought Maria. The annoying pre-run pep talk. It was the second week of the training program, and hers was the lone voice unheard in the cheer. How many times was she going to have to stand there and listen to this nonsense? It took a particular sort of person to race in excess of four hours, the equivalent of half a workday, with chaffing between the legs, and a brain turned to stun by prolonged lack of glycogen.

From across the room, Grace sent a sympathetic half-smile.

Maria and Grace were surprised to have found each other both signed up for marathon training. Wordlessly, they agreed not to breathe a word about their past, and instead put one foot in front of the other.

Fifteen lost souls gathered in the windowless backroom of the running store, breathing stuffy air. Maria doubted even one of them knew what they were really up against. The collapsible tables used for seminars and other gatherings were pushed against the wall, the plastic chairs stacked neatly nearby.

When Maria signed up for the training program, she'd told herself it was the only way to fill in the missing pieces. There had to be some reason she'd been unable to complete the distance in the past. She was willing to open herself to fresh ideas. Really, she was.

But the woman with the blue bandana had them yanking on cold muscles. Forward folds, quad stretches, shoulder shrugs, and heaven-save-us-all calf pulls. Show some respect, would ya? Did she even know what calves do? The calves are a second heart. A frigging miracle of engineering, they hold a reservoir of blood. When a calf muscle contracts, blood is pumped up the leg against gravity. The calves are vital to running for so many reasons, plus they are always too tight and easily torn. Anyone who knew anything knew that.

While the rest of the class lined up against the wall, pressing against the unmoveable surface, pushing away with one leg bent and the other stretched, Maria was a conscientious objector. She put herself into the approximate shape of everyone else, except she kept enough bend in her outstretched leg to protect her calf.

A glance to the side revealed the stringy-haired blonde with a crinkly mouth, who Maria had noticed several times before, was doing the same.

Hanna decided to run a marathon the day she watched the annual Welltown race. They hold it at the same time as the cowboy festival while the city streets are loaded with tourists in pointy-toed boots and rolled-brim hats. She'd been out of rehab a year and was clean as the mountain river tumbling over mottled grey rocks.

Some people she'd noticed ran the forty-two kilometres solo, but most were teamed up in little clusters of two or three, joined by a radically harsh goal. The audacity of it. Three hours into the race, she'd caught them laughing, red in the face and sweaty. She'd hopped on the city train to witness them later at the finish line—not the top runners but the older, less-trim ordinary folk like her. Most people watched the weary bodies crossing the line. She was more interested in the finishers' chute. People hugging away and high-fiving.

Later, when later she saw a listing in the campus news rag where she worked, she'd thought she'd like to try. Maybe she could laugh, red in the face and sweaty, high-five at the finish, break her some rules. Crazy, really, given that she'd never run anywhere before, unless you call racing after a bus pulling from the curb "running."

And now, she was doing it, or so she claimed. But from the start, Hanna felt out of place. First day of the training program, she'd glanced around the backroom of the running store, confirming her worst suspicions. The others were mostly all young, with readily repairing muscles and the recklessness that goes with such flesh. At fifty-two, what did she bring to the task? Cranky hips and a stiff lower back.

She'd been watching Maria awhile. The woman was stubborn and slim, uppity if you wanted to be exact, and mature. Deep creases marked the corners of her hawkish eyes, her lips were thin, and she stood off to the side in her own special world. It seemed to Hanna that maybe Maria knew things.

When Maria refused the calf stretch, she did the same. And later, when partway through the prescribed ten-kilometre run/ walk in the second week of the program, Maria veered off in a whole new direction, away from the pod of fifteen unmatched bodies pretending they were compatible, clomping lock-step down the narrow river pathway? Well, it was practically a no-brainer. Hanna followed.

Grace would tell anyone who thought to ask that her goal was simple. She only wanted to cover the distance. It'd be plenty, she argued, if she could feel the weight of a finisher medal over her breasts. Honestly, whose business was it anyway?

Jayden had started dating a younger saleswoman who competed in triathlons. Apparently, they'd met on the job. He'd asked Grace for a divorce. And Brianne, her long-time exercise buddy, was off on a different continent, making the world a better place with her adorable freckled-faced husband. They were building schools and hospitals in Ghana, caving and rock climbing in their spare time, visiting entire villages built on stilts, watching elephants and counting bird species.

Two weeks into the running program, the runners were playing follow-the-leader on the narrow pathway that barely accommodated two bodies in motion side-by-side. With Tribute Drive to their right and the river to their left, they formed an impenetrable blockade to anyone on foot heading towards them. Cyclists whooshed past on the parallel pathway. Pedestrians brash enough to have imagined the hoard would allow them through ended up stepping aside onto the grass.

"Keep it in the comfort zone," said their fearless leader in the blue bandana. "Remember, you should be able to hold a conversation without getting out of breath." Talking was what the runners did best. Such a racket, they did not hear the protests of pedestrians forced off the path.

Grace was happy, more or less, in the caboose, where she kept company with the seventy-something guy and the other woman carrying a few extra pounds. To the constant roar of traffic and the drone of voices, they trotted along. The guy was not a big talker, but the other woman . . . holy, wow. After only a couple of runs, Grace already knew the names of all the woman's children, co-workers, and siblings.

Struggling with eating and your "relationship with food," as they called it in group, could leave a person feeling like a freak and a loser. Ha, to that Slimmer You. So there. A new way of reducing. But seriously, a body could not stop eating. The substance with which Grace was held in an unhealthy bond was not something she could ever forsake.

Maria had to understand. Although they'd never spoken of it, they shared more than their bodies might suggest. Maria was looking much better these days, some colour in her skin, some meat on her bones. And yet, the refusal to join in, the isolation and privacy. Grace couldn't help but feel concerned. When Maria ran out of line in her own direction, cutting ties, Grace followed.

"Wait up," she called out. Maria and that other woman stopped briefly, waving her in.

Maria never asked to be their leader. A few hundred metres from where they broke away, running Rambo-style over the grass, not even on a pathway, Maria saw a footbridge, and they took it. On the other side of the river, the three women escaped the exhaust fumes and the crinkling white noise of relentless traffic, and the wonk-wonk of too many people talking. Now, they could hear themselves think. And, contrary to instinct, noted Maria, thinking was part of running. Yet another reason that person in charge of the training program was a moron.

"Hope it's okay I joined you," said the stringy-haired blonde with a crinkly lip. They'd been running together away from the herd for several minutes and the woman was keeping up, although she was breathing hard. Grace, too, had butted in and was trotting alongside. "I'm a newbie to this running stuff," the woman added. "Never done a single race. My name's Hanna."

"We all start somewhere." A secret bubble of joy expanded Maria's rib cage. Her lungs filled with cleaner air. Beginners were such good company. "Nice to meet you. I'm Maria."

"Didn't want you setting out alone," said Grace, patting Maria on the shoulder, tottering a little. "Not after all we've been through together. I used to be Maria's boss," she told Hanna, with a show-off tilt of her look-at-me-I'm-important head.

So much for giving each other freedom from an ugly past. Briefly, Maria's focus was taken away from running. Precious energy leaked through her feet like wet marks on the asphalt, memories of what never was. You're not the bloody boss of me, woman, Maria thought to herself. And this was precisely why thinking mattered so much.

A body needed to know what it was doing, especially when running. Maria refocused on one foot after the other.

Anyway, Grace had a weighty load on those narrow ankles. If Maria had veered only a little to the side during the unwelcome moment of supervision, her former boss would have toppled. Power came from within; that was certain.

Hanna lined herself up according to the standard set by Maria. The stopwatch started, and her right foot pushed off, propelling her forward. They'd been doing their own version of marathon training for over a week now.

Soon, Grace was panting to save her life, and Maria was practically silent. Seriously annoying. If it weren't for the steady tap of that woman's too-delicate feet, they might not know Maria was running.

Speed-work was not part of a beginner's training program, and Hanna had not wanted to do it. It came with too great a risk of injury, and beginners were better served by focusing on distance, or so they'd been told in the backroom of the running store.

"Balderdash," said Maria. "Speed-work teaches the body what it needs to do. You'll know what I mean when you feel it."

And Hanna did. As she flung herself into the next moment, her legs felt longer, her back straighter, her mind clearer. She lifted her chin, raised her chest and opened her heart. For a moment, she was once again a barefoot girl in a sundress, running over dewy lawns, crossing the front yards of every house on the block, laughing with a girlfriend on either side.

Maybe it was the wind pushing her hair back. Maybe it was the restlessness in her legs, their urgent need to run for their life. Hanna's feet wanted to float, and so she let them.

She was not thinking about Maria or Grace when she bolted ahead solo, her face slicked with sweat. For reasons she didn't understand, breathing came easier with speed. Her blood filled with happy hormones, not so unfamiliar, the undeniable buoyancy of a chemically-enhanced moment. Hello, she thought, I know you. Welcome back, it's been too long.

The stopwatch beeped, and it was over. Hanna took a few more steps, stopped, and turned around with her hands braced on her knees. Now, at last, she was breathing hard, catching up on what she'd been missing. Her lungs were raw. Her throat burned. She looked to the side, hoping for approval. Here we come, she'd thought, the high-fives.

But Maria glowered. "What on earth do you think you're doing?"

A gazillion itty-bitty needles pricked Hanna's skin up and down her exposed arms and legs. All the joy sunk into the warped asphalt, buckled from deep frosts and rapid thaws.

She felt deflated and useless, unable to straighten up, unable to catch her breath. "I'm sorry," she mumbled.

"Didn't I say we need to maintain a stable speed?" asked Maria. "That's how people get injured."

Hanna had finished well ahead of Maria. She'd clearly been fastest. So why did she feel inferior? "I'll do better next time," Hanna choked.

Even as she'd posed to run the first speed interval of her life, getting too much advice from Maria, and already feeling sick, Grace knew she'd never keep up. Three steps in, Hanna and Maria had already left her behind. Each minute that passed took them farther away.

Hanna's hair had whooshed, a wash of dirty blond freed by the wind, the back of her head its own show of power. And Maria, with that effortless stride, she might as well have been running at an easy pace. Neither woman had been the slightest bit aware of how Grace was struggling.

Part of her had wanted to walk. If she'd refused to try, she might have reclaimed a shred of dignity. But she'd lifted her vague chin and kept trotting, wobbly bits everywhere, heavy-footed and scared. She'd not been fast, but, yeah, she was steady. And soon, she'd been nauseous, close to throwing up the plain toast and single egg she'd had for breakfast. The tiny glass of grapefruit juice she'd allowed herself as a treat had become acid wash at the back of her throat.

She must have been out of her blessed mind to think for one measly second that she could do this. A tiny squirt of hot urine had leaked into the special runner panties Grace bought from the store on the first day of training. She looked down to see if there was a stain, grateful there was not.

When Grace finally caught up, neither woman noticed her approaching. They were having a spat from the look of things, although Grace had too much going on to catch the substance of the conversation. It was only when she made light of the situation that the other women included her.

"Hey, you two," she said. "Settle down. This isn't a race."

Burning up with over-exertion, Grace pressed the base of her palm to the bottom of her rib cage, grimacing.

"Side stitch?" asked Maria. "Here's what we do." She positioned herself in front of Grace, commanding all her attention. With her lips puckered into a narrow tube, Maria pushed a long *shooo* out her mouth. "Force all the air out . . . hard but gradual," she said after the demonstration. "Keep breathing out as long as you can. Strong and steady."

Grace did as she was told. As best as she could, she emptied her lungs by way of force. Okay, truth. She channelled her repressed anger into the grand reservoir of strength she'd worked years building. Because, damn, a person could be larger and still have muscle. Three long exhales at maximum force, and the side stitch was gone.

"No worries. Happens to me too," said Maria. "Usually towards the end of a long run when I'm most tired."

It was a month and a half until the race, and Maria stepped out of bed to teeth-grinding pain. Her right foot was planted, but she was reluctant to put weight on her left. The carpet offered insufficient cushion for her tender foot as she did a hippity-hop to her galley kitchen in the one-bedroom apartment to make herself a high-protein breakfast of peanut butter on a whole-wheat bagel, with a bit of honey for endurance.

She had to start warming up slowly, or she would keep worsening the damage. She knew the tissue on the bottom of her foot was basically a series of fat rubber bands extending from each heel towards the toes. The plantar fascia elongates and contracts to support the arch and enable normal foot mechanics. On the dominant side, hers were brittle with microscopic tears, countless super-tiny locations of damage.

In tissue that does not get enough blood, repair is slow. She immersed her right foot in ice water for twenty-minute intervals every evening and before work in the morning. All those nerve endings screeching at her madness, she'd have done anything to avoid another failed attempt. She'd been careful. Nightly massages with her running stick, stretching like it was her religion. She did not understand why this kept happening to her.

But, as she observed and self-corrected, Maria saw a way through. After her bagel had been smeared with peanut butter, as she poured herself a tall mug of black coffee, she noticed her foot hurt less. As she ate, she walked around her living room. Each step on the dominant side was a bit looser. Heading to her car, she told herself she was practically pain-free.

But the fascias do not do well with rest. Those rubber bands contract, shrink back, tighten like cowardly would-be people

Maria does not want to know. And when she got out of her car at their meeting point in the parking lot beside the out-of-the-way theatre in an old pumphouse, she was forcing herself to perform a normal gait.

Grace smelled of lavender shampoo, her face shining with a recent application of moisturizer. Hanna had on a white running cap turned backwards and sunglasses with blue-tinted wraparound lenses on her do-as-I-please face.

They were scheduled to complete twenty-seven kilometres on the sweltering summer morning, hoping to finish before noon, and Maria refused to believe the pain would persist. All she needed was to take it slow.

"Hey, Grace," she said, "How about you lead? At least for the first ten. You can keep us honest. It's important not to do these long runs too fast."

Maria turned to Hanna, "Don't forget to stretch those shins after we warm up. It's all about avoiding injury at this point. After our first three, during the walk break, we'll stop to stretch. Okay?"

"Gotcha, Coach. Good idea," said Hanna.

Maria's heart swelled. She loved being called "Coach," absolutely she did. And she deserved the title. She'd studied running with devotion. How many people knew the hours she'd put into it? She knew what the other women had yet to learn. Able to cool through sweat, in possession of powerhouse glutes, at ease breathing through the mouth, and equipped with fabulously light forearms—the human body is perfect for long-distance running.

On the quiet side of the river, the path wound through poplar trees and open grass scattered with pink paintbrushes and white daisies holding bright yellow suns. Every now and then, a red-winged blackbird flared its wings, opened its black beak, and let loose a glorious trill.

There was a pull in gradual progress, the deliberate calculation of success. There was an undeniable forward momentum in repetition that led to improvement, three-speed intervals and then four, fourteen kilometres and then sixteen.

Maria was eating more, no denying it. Nuts by the handful, honey-coated sesame seeds anytime she wanted, a six-inch, whole-wheat sub stuffed with tuna and veg after every long run, before she went home to an ice bath.

At twenty kilometres, they stopped to pee, taking turns in the log-style outhouse identified by a sign with a line drawing of a woman in a triangular dress.

"How you holding out?" Grace asked Maria in a hushed voice, when Hanna was busy using the outhouse. That familiar look of concern, the need to intervene, and the way Grace pretended to understand. Mind your own business, thought Maria. You've problems of your own. And if I needed help, I'd ask for it.

Later, near the end of their run, when salty sweat caked Maria's face, and her muscles were long since done, Grace said to Maria, again when Hanna was out of earshot, "I think you're limping."

Their thirty-two kilometres started with clouds in the sky, dimming the cruel sun. The poplar leaves rattled in the wind. A great horned owl swooped over their heads. Hanna never dreamt she would make it this far. With less than a month of training remaining, she was starting to believe she might actually run a marathon.

"Would ya look at us?" she said. "Two long runs before the race and doing well. None of us injured. We're gonna make it!"

Maria was wearing new shoes. Their white was pristine. Neon-green racing stripes marked the outside heels. Dark sunglasses shielded her eyes, making it hard to guess what she might be feeling. Hanna had noted a limp and decided not to say anything. Could it be the mighty coach was not as unbreakable as she pretended?

Grace had on a grey shirt with black lettering that proclaimed, "Life's short. Running makes it longer." Her matching white cap rested snuggly over blond curls. There was a peachy glow to her skin.

They took a final pre-run pee in the outhouse next to the parking lot at the bottom of the valley. They'd travelled to the winding park at the edge of Welltown because the park offered more shade and variety for what was likely to be more than four hours of running.

Hanna had told neither woman of her irritations. The slow burn started in the final stretch of a long run a month earlier, and it had been gradually getting worse, the angry red spreading over her inner thighs, more after every run. She could no longer wear a bathing suit for the shame of it. Soaking in a cool tub made her shiver. Diaper cream worked on babies but only made a gooey mess on her. And forget about loose-fitting shorts. They only brought the sore spots into direct contact, increasing the friction at the delicate skin between her inner thighs, a part of the female body that was forever touching.

In the early kilometres, mild air wiped the smallest sign of sweat from Hanna's skin, and her thighs did not rub. She'd smeared enough sports glide on them. Maybe this time, it would last. The pathway was crowded with clusters of other runners too carefree to be going long. Meanwhile, baby carriages pulled their parents, forming blockages, slowing everyone down.

At the three-quarter mark, Hanna's feet became tender. Her energy drained at a rate too fast to be recharged by electrolyte pouches of pudding-like substance, and very bad things happened below. The ongoing abrasion between her legs weakened her carefully constructed facade of positivity, which made her say stupid things. *Oh, look at us still doing it. Aren't we wonderful? Rah-rah.* Dark thoughts threatened to throw her off the nearest bridge into the glacially-fed river.

No matter how Hanna strained to catch up, Maria was always a few steps ahead, clomping along in her uneven gait, pretending to be stronger than she was. What broke the longing, the insane need to pursue? Maybe it was simple exhaustion. Maybe, it was rage. But it landed like sobriety, shaky and resolute. When Hanna's legs turned sluggish, she allowed them.

A minute later, Grace was beside her. Blisteringly red in the face with wet stains under her armpits, Grace's feet dragged on the hot asphalt. She took a quick slug of water before trying to talk. "How you doing, Hanna? Wanna take a walk break? It's okay if you're tired."

Thirty-five kilometres? They must have been insane. And would it have killed Hanna and Maria to stop once in a while to check if Grace was okay? She was doing it same as them, yet they treated her like a lost cause, chugging along at the back of the line.

Now that they were nearing race day, Grace entertained fantasies about making it across the finish line. *Beep-beep. Roar. Lookee me, I did it.* Jayden was going to eat his shirt. Wait till he found out what she'd done. She'd divorce him nonetheless.

But please, oh please, could somebody make her nipples stop bleeding? This was not an ache or a dull tingle from a nick to the finger. This was clothespin twisting. Hallelujah, Mother of All, it was ungodly.

The other women could never have begun to comprehend, what with their tidy breasts the size of marshmallows. Grace had been cursed with back aches her entire life, an anatomical misalignment, stresses she'd never been built to sustain. Running made everything worse.

She should never have listened to Maria. Yes, the woman had read a lot of books, and she subscribed to that idiot magazine, but she did not know everything.

"Sports glide," Maria suggested glibly, like they were talking about chapped lips. "Or nip guards, that'll help." Did she even know what those were? Had she ever laid eyes upon a pair?

Some jackass scientist, male, no doubt, came up with those innocent-looking instruments of torture. Yes, they stopped nipples from bleeding, at least while they were on, but those suckers caused a circular rash around the edges of their seal.

Remove them, and Grace's nipples leaked blood. And now, each nipple was marked by an angry red circle, perfect ugly bull's eyes, one on either side.

When Grace had followed Maria all those months earlier, leaving behind the training program she'd paid for, she'd only wanted to make sure Maria was okay. She'd never signed up for hours and hours of pure unmitigated misery. Two kilometres from the end of their gruelling long run, Grace watched Maria disappear around the curve in the pathway where even Try-Harder Hanna was unable to keep up.

And the race, heaven help them, would be farther still. Seven body-destroying kilometres farther, in front of a crowd of enthusiastic watchers, as eager to see misery as they were to witness triumph. Almost five months of raw lungs and bleeding nipples, never being able to keep up with her so-called running partners, feeling perpetually not good enough, Grace was ready to raise her hands and stop this nonsense. Jayden didn't know she'd been training. Plus, there was something horrifically wrong with her body, how the quads clenched, how the calves had become so tightly strung they were ready to snap, how the small of her back groaned, how her nipples screamed.

Then Hanna slowed. They were side-by-side, neither better than the other.

"Hey, you alright?" Grace asked, looking at Hanna's sad face.

Their weary feet slapped the asphalt path. Their arms no longer swung but hung like useless anchors too short to reach the ground. She dared not check her GPS in case the remaining distance registered in her flesh as too much to survive.

"One cranky foot. Then the other. Repeat," said Hanna with a bitter laugh.

"Oh, heavens. Truly. Is it really that simple?" A rush of heat rose through Grace's baked flesh and escaped out the top of her head. Her feet became lighter. "What are you going to do after we're done?" she asked Hanna. They were old friends now, sharing secrets. "Me? I'm having a big tuna sandwich and a bit of dark chocolate. And then, I don't care what time it is, I'm going to bed. Delicious cool cotton sheets with the curtains drawn to black."

"Likewise," said Hanna. "Bed sounds perfect."

After the alarm went off, for a few precious minutes, Maria forgot she could not run the race. The date was stored in her angry muscles, formed from small acts of damage caused by ongoing strain. Her quads bulged above the knees, her calves held fists, and her glutes were monsters. But her left foot would not stand.

Try as she might, she could no longer fake a normal stride. Even walking, she dipped and wrenched whenever she tried to put weight on her dominant foot. The pacesetter, the forward stepper, refused now to take orders. It shrunk back in a knot of anguish. Her leader had forsaken her.

For ten long days, she'd hardly left her apartment. The insurance company where she'd now been working for two years was threatening to fire her. She needed the job. It'd not been easy to find. After the incident with the ambulance, the whole campus watching as they took her away on a stretcher with a pee stain between her legs and a broken spine, she could not have returned to her job at the college. It had made no difference how long Grace held it for her.

She dressed herself in ordinary jeans and a t-shirt, put her long-billed running cap on, and laced the pristine shoes. If she'd rested when the injury started, it might have healed. If she hadn't pushed too hard on that last run.

The four-lane downtown street was crowded with people who were better than she would ever be. Strong-jawed women with no makeup under their running caps. Men in tights and wicking tank tops. She didn't seriously expect to find Grace and Hanna among the thousand bodies gathered at the starting line for the marathon, each wearing a numbered tag on their chest. But later, if either woman asked, she could say she'd tried.

From the makeshift stage at the front, on scaffolding to allow runners safe passage underneath, bad disco blared. A woman with a bright blue ponytail and branded athletic wear led the crowd through a warm-up no one was doing. Hobbling, Maria made her way towards the back of the line until her foot protested so loudly she had to find a cement flowerpot to sit upon. The narrow edge cut into her bottom. The morning air was colder in the shade of office towers, and it chilled her to the bone. She tugged her running cap over her face, shielding her stinging eyes.

The voice was too familiar to pretend they were strangers. "Maria!" From within the huddle of ready-to-go runners, three minutes from the gun, Hanna squeezed her way through to the sidewalk, quite possibly losing her position. "Maria! Coach! It's good seeing you."

Grace was at her side, smelling of lavender shampoo, looking fresh and more muscular than Maria remembered. "Thanks for coming, Coach. Means a lot."

The smallest bubble of joy burst before it came anywhere near Maria's heart. In its place, a backwash of stomach acid. "Wanted to wish both of you luck," she said in a gruff voice. Then she gave each of her running partners a clutch-and-release hug before pushing them away. "Get back in line! You don't have much time."

The gun popped, the crowd cheered, and precious little happened. For several minutes, hyped-up runners lifted a knee and planted a foot, lifted the other and planted the other, in a clownish mimicry of actual running. Amongst the log-jam of bodies, nobody was going anywhere fast.

Hanna chomped on the anxiety of a decision she'd made months earlier. She was here, the race had begun, yet she was unsure she could do it. *Too late now, sucker. And, yikes, look at all the people watching.*

Fifteen minutes later, the crowd thinned enough that she could hear the pat of Grace's feet. Their legs moved in unison, and she started to feel better. Maybe she would finish strong. Maybe she would fly through the inflatable red arch at the end. She would high-five complete strangers, hug her loyal son. Kyle was such a good boy. She was blessed.

"We're ready for this," said Grace. "Think of all the hours training."

"Ah, yeah, if I'd actually known what I was getting into, I'd probably never have started. But gosh, oh wow, it's a kick being here."

Barrel-chested guys in their twenties, snowy-haired women with sleek legs, the exquisitely tall and the pear-shaped. Humans were herd animals, and people made way for each other, carried one another along, formed a collective. The shape you came in did not matter so long as you could keep going.

Hanna had told Grace about the addiction and recovery, how she'd needed to show herself that she was more. This was the first time she'd taken on something really hard by choice. During the two-week taper before the race, her chaffing had caked over in blood, turned into funny speckled scabbing and gradually healed. Doubtlessly, it had helped that she'd chosen to go bottomless at home. Ah my, the things we did for running.

At twenty-five kilometres, walking and sipping water, swallowing the foul-tasting pouch of pudding that balances her electrolytes, Hanna completed an honest and fearless inventory. Yes, she listened to her heartbeat. Yes, she checked the rhythm of her breathing. Yes, she observed with care the state of her calves and thighs. And she discovered, to great wonder, that she did not feel tired.

And then, around about thirty-five kilometres, they stepped through an invisible curtain into an entirely different reality. Her legs filled with cement, her feet dragged. She could no longer catch her breath, and a side stitch knifed her under the ribs. All this, although she was moving so slowly, an able-bodied person could have passed her walking.

The sun was high in the sky, belting down on her Marilyn Monroe skin. Her blond curls were wet with sweat. Her numbered bib was crinkled from all the times she'd reached across for water or a nose rag.

At thirty-seven kilometres, as they trudged up a wisp of a hill, Grace turned to Hanna and said, "One cranky foot." Huff. "Then the other." Huff. "Repeat." Huff. "Isn't that what you said?" The joke still worked on Grace.

But Hanna had retreated to the darkness inside her. She did not answer. At this point in the race, all the remaining runners had blinders on. The faster people had long since gone home. Those still slogging were not in the mood. "Hey, stay off the road," they snarled to fans who'd seen what they came for and were leaving. "There's still a race on. Geesh."

Grace shuffled forward on tender feet. The nails on her big toes got hammered with each step. Probably, she was going to lose them. She'd found a better sports bra, so at least the nipples weren't that bad. It was the small of her back whining incessantly. Plus, her hips felt weirdly stiff, as if she had on a too-tight girdle.

They'd passed the forty-kilometre mark when her right calf twisted in an excruciatingly tight knot. "Ow!" she wailed. "Ow!" She balanced precariously on a single foot, the cramped leg curled back in would-be protection except it did nothing to help.

Hanna sidled over. Grace hadn't known she was so close. "Here," she said. "Lean on me."

Grace clutched Hanna's shoulder, forcing her friend to carry extra weight. "Cramp in my calf," she wailed, telling herself to stop burdening Hanna, unable to let go of the support. "God above, I don't know if I can take anymore. Better go on without me."

"No, I won't leave you."

Grace felt an arm wrap over her back and under her armpit, bracing her soundly.

"We started together. We'll finish the same way."

With a growl through gritting teeth, Grace put all her weight on the cramping leg. She pressed down into the ball of her foot. Slowly breathing in, she lingered in the tightness, and the pain began to lessen.

They moved forward, each step a little less uncertain. Hanna did not press the pace. Their ragged breaths kind of matched. Their heavy feet landed in unison. At the sound of a crowd cheering at the finish line, those true fans remaining, something opened up inside of Grace, a surge of pride inside her ribs.

Together, they sprinted. The rubber padding over the electronic sensor under the finish line was extra soft. For a split second, they flew. *Beep-beep. Clapping. Lookee us. Oh my God, we did it!*

The friends embraced in the finisher's chute, holding onto each other for dear life, or at least until their breathing returned to normal. A volunteer congratulated Grace, leaning in with a bright smile. And finally, good gracious, not a moment too soon, Grace felt the full weight of a medal over her breasts.

Sundowning

In the upstairs room of her parent's home, Pauline stands at attention before her father's mahogany desk. Murky light creeps in through the window. Her fist holds a wad of cash.

Through the heavy silence, a voice creaks behind her, "You're nothing but a stinking thief."

Over her shoulder, she sees the sagging cheeks of a sharp-eyed woman. "It's okay, Mom. I was clearing away Dad's things. Remember, I told you, we have to go through his papers."

He hadn't said a word to Pauline, not in forty years, not a letter, not a phone call. He'd been through chemo and radiation and a stay in hospice, months of knowing the end was near, and he never once found the spine to reckon with the harm he'd caused. A judge, anyone might think, would have some sense of justice. But the greatest father of all time walked away scot-free, naming Pauline executor of his estate.

"Don't pretend I can't see what you're doing, Pauline. Where'd you get that money?"

Pauline's thumb rubs the edge of the stack. The crisp new bills snap. Like many things in her parents' life, there's no way to explain it. Her mother never had any job other than being the wife of a big shot. Mrs. Shaw allowed that man to control everything.

"Don't stand there looking *stupific*. I'm not a fool, you know." Her mother's jaw moves like she's chewing food, her eyelids lower, and for a moment, her expression freezes. "Are you stupid, girl?" She's been doing that a lot lately, messing up words and fixing them as if there's a five-second rule for dropping the wrong syllable. Change it fast enough, and it's still safe to put in your mouth.

"It was at the back of his desk. Who keeps this much cash laying around? You'd think he'd be more careful." The desk drawer is still open, and Pauline considers tucking the money back where she found it. If she moves fast enough, maybe her mother will forget what she saw. Later, when her mother's not watching, Pauline can go back and retrieve the cash without causing a fuss.

Dusk is the hardest time of day. The fading light worsens the confusion, makes her mother do things she'd never have done before. Her mother has forgotten to do up all the buttons on her mauve shirt. Peekaboo glimpses of skin and a faded bra show through the gaps.

"Don't play innocent with me, missy. You've been going through my stuff and taking things. First, you tricked me into letting you into the study. Now you're stealing from me."

Pauline clenches her jaw, shakes her head. "For crying out loud, Mom. Stop this nonsense. Listen to what you're saying."

A bony finger jabs Pauline's face. "I'm going to call the police. I'm going to have you arrested."

Slapping the wad of cash into her mother's hand, Pauline says, "Fine then, take it."

Her mother's face turns ash white, the cheeks droop, the mouth slops open. Gone again, Mrs. Shaw is out of contact. The supposed nurturer, the supposed safe lap to rest upon, has once again fled.

Staring at the Persian rug, Pauline has her back against the cold wall. She hates the way her body freezes in moments that call for action. If she had any courage in her at all, she'd simply vamoose.

And then, like a blessed light shining down, an honest, plain miracle. Who knows why her mother's faraway mind glimmers awake, so bright-eyed and fully on.

All of that motherly attention lands on Pauline. Such a delicious thrill, it sparkles in her brain. A warm puddle forms around her heart. She cannot stop herself.

Over the years, Pauline did try to stay in contact. They'd had secret meetings in the park, coffee in quiet neighbourhoods, late-night phone calls. When even those stopped, she'd figured her mother had done what she always did. She'd backed away and turned silent. But if Pauline had been in closer touch, she'd have known her mother was having problems.

In her own defence, Pauline had been going through a few problems herself—divorce, for instance, starting over in her fifties, for example, thinking she'd expelled her painful childhood but finding out there was more inside her. So much for all that. She's face-to-face with it now, and her daughter is right at her side.

She'd never asked Emma to interrupt her studies, but when that girl sees a problem, she has to step in. Same thing happened when Pauline and Oliver divorced. Emma moved in with her dad so he wouldn't be alone. She'd only just recently managed to break free and restart her own life.

Emma's doing a master's in social work. Her thesis is on Alzheimer's, and she claims this is an opportunity for research. Pauline can't deny that Emma brings an air of calm to the impossible situation. After the incident with the cash, there's nothing Pauline can do to settle her mother. Then Emma returns, and within minutes, she has Mrs. Shaw resting easy in her favourite wingback chair in front of a nature show on TV.

Pauline returns to the study, determined to finish. The sooner she settles her father's accounts, the sooner she can decide what to do about her mother, and Emma can return to her studies. Pauline is old enough to get a senior's discount some places. It's high time everybody forgot what happened to her as a child. No matter how long she stands at attention at his desk, her father will never come up behind her. But the feeling is the same, gasping for breath, holding it at the back of her nose like a warning, tiny shivers at the sides of her face, tingles along her lips.

Most kids were spanked in their own room on their own bed. Pauline took her punishment on her feet, in her father's study, bent over the antique mahogany desk with swirly grain-like crushed fur and cup-style pull handles made of brass. Afterwards, Pauline would be sent to bed without anything to eat, alone until morning, as if her very existence was something to be kept out of sight.

And where was her mother during all this, a person might wonder. Folding warm sheets in the laundry? Reading a paperback in the library? Sorting the canned goods in their pantry? Pauline would not see her mother's small-mouthed face until darkness had fallen, and her mother had finally mustered the courage to creep into her daughter's room wearing a velour housecoat.

Perched on the edge of Pauline's bed, her mother sang, "Fly Me to the Moon," as if it were a secret only the two of them shared. Her mother's voice reclaimed Pauline's body, her muscle, all her soft tissues, the smallest bones. The quivering recognition of having once been a single inseparable being, the feeling of warmth.

Her mother had been a professional singer before she got married. With the last three words of the song, she leaned close to Pauline. "I love you," she sang, and kissed Pauline's forehead. And then she was gone.

Alone in the dark room with tree shadows looming on the blinds over her window, Pauline tried to keep the fleeting sense of comfort from the days before she'd lost her childhood, when she still believed she had a mother and was safe in the world.

But all that remained in her cold room was the scent of her mother's perfume, lily of the valley with a trail of jasmine. The perfume was fresh, clear and blindingly false. Her mother never mentioned what he did. She never said it was wrong; she never tried to stop him.

There was more than enough money to put her mother into a good home. According to the websites, Mrs. Shaw could have a private studio with mountain views, stimulating programs, a spa, a beauty salon, a fitness centre and attentive staff. They called the services they provide "memory care." But what does her mother remember? She was never there.

Pauline dumps the last of the contents from her father's desk into the trash, turning each drawer upside down, watching the contents tumble. The important papers are safely stored in a box. And the wad of cash Pauline slapped into her mother's hand? It's probably stuffed in the white cardigan her mother had been wearing. By morning, her mother will have forgotten it's there.

When Pauline stops by the kitchen to say goodbye to Emma, her mother is still watching giraffes eating leaves from tall trees. There are elephants nearby. A tiger lurks amongst shadows in the yellow grass.

"Think I'll be going," Pauline says, buttoning her jacket.

Emma turns from the stove. "Okay. I'll take it from here."

The girl should be at home making her own dinner or hanging out with friends, not here in this big lonesome house with an angry woman accusing people of things they'd never do.

Pauline's trembling hands find the car keys at the bottom of her purse.

"Wait a minute," Emma says. "One more thing." She goes to the kitchen, where the white cardigan is still hanging over a chair. She digs into the pockets and retrieves the missing cash. "Quick. Take this away."

Pauline stuffs the money into her open purse, thinking that will be the end of it.

Although the TV continues to blare in the adjoining room, all this time her mother must have been listening. Mrs. Shaw marches herself into the room with her chin jutting out. "What do you have in that purse, Pauline?"

Before Pauline can get away, her mother rips the purse off her shoulder. Pauline's belongings scatter onto the floor: lipstick and tissues, her wallet and cell phone, pens, a small coiled notebook . . . plus all that cash drifting around like so much paper waste.

Mrs. Shaw's hands look surprisingly dainty. Emma's painted the nails a warm shade of peach. Delicately on her knees, Mrs. Shaw collects the bills, one at a time, lining them up in a neat stack on the floor. A frothy bubble of whitish spittle clings to her bottom lip.

"This does not *beebong* to you. It's not yours. Don't take things that aren't yours!"

Pauline watches as Emma joins in the effort to collect the money, then helps Mrs. Shaw back onto her feet. The two of them form a cocoon of mutual attention that shuts everyone else out. At university, Emma took a course that teaches an approach called Validation. According to Emma, it's the best way to help people with Alzheimer's.

"You think this money was stolen?"

"I know it."

"The money is important to you."

"All my life, people have been taking things from me. I only want what's rightfully mine. Is that too much to ask?"

"No, it isn't."

Pauline watches her mother's frown melt away, her liver-coloured mouth curling into a genuine smile. "Thank you, my sweet girl," she says to Emma.

As a child, Pauline remembers her mother was always in the kitchen, traipsing from stove to sink to counter, making pot roast, lasagna or, Pauline's favourite, shepherd's pie. Steam lifted off the potatoes mashed with butter and cream. Her mother fried the hamburger with onions, a splash of dry red wine, baby peas, and carrots cut into tiny cubes. The top was coated with sharp cheddar that browned extra dark in the oven.

Her mother wore dresses too fancy for a homemaker. Sometimes Pauline wondered, was that her mother's one act of defiance? Even now, Pauline can see the outfits. How she'd studied them as a girl, imagining her scrawny frame in her mother's best clothes, hoping, one day, she could be that beautiful. The yellow polka-dotted swing dress, wow. And the red bouffant with the sweetheart neckline. Her mother liked wearing that one with pearls. But, best of all, the most special, was her mother's blue velvet number with a wide collar over the shoulders and the tucked-in waist with a matching rose, also velvet, pinned at the side.

Most of the time, her mother's dresses were hidden under pinafore aprons. The aprons were every bit as impressive as the dresses. Pink with white polka dots, navy blue with daisy accents, ruffled pockets and floppy strings tied at the back in extravagant bows.

Children will believe all sorts of nonsense—Santa, gnomes, fairies. A skinny thing in white leotards and plaid shift dresses, Pauline was no different. She believed a single look from her mother was all she needed to withstand the heavy brow of her father's disapproval and what so often came later.

She'd follow her mother around the kitchen. When her mother lingered at the stove, she'd line up behind her. She'd stand on one foot, hoping to be noticed as if it was a magic spell, and if only she kept her balance, if only she didn't wobble, her mother would turn. Those green eyes would awaken, the freckles on her mother's cheeks would rise, and the corners of her mouth would curl, all for her little girl.

A week passes as Pauline tries to get Emma to agree it's time to put Mrs. Shaw into care. Emma's been entertaining the notion of taking care of her grandmother for several more months, or even a year. She's encouraged by a few small moments of calm. Then something bad happens, as Pauline knew it would.

"Is your mother Helen Shaw?"

At the sound of her mother's name, Pauline presses the phone closer. She is at the registrar counter at the local college, doing her job. Prospective students are lined up, waiting for assistance. "Yes."

"There's been a bit of upset with your mom," the man says slowly.

Ever since Pauline came back into contact with her mother, she'd been waiting for this to happen. She expected a call to come from the police, or worse, the hospital. She never expected the call to come from a financial institution and a guy who says he's a client care representative.

"We have her in a quiet room," the man says. "But your mother needs a ride home. She was having a few challenges with the bank machine. When staff tried to help, she grew flustered." He clears his throat, lowers his voice, "We had to intervene."

Pauline gets a colleague to take over at the registrar counter, and she rushes to the bank. But by the time she arrives, her mother is as demure as she was on trips through the city to see the dentist or doctor when Pauline was a child. Such occasions called for a mink coat and sunglasses. Her mother has neither fashion item now, only a beige trench coat and ordinary silver-rimmed reading glasses perched too far down her nose.

They have given her mother a cup of tea. She's sipping from a Styrofoam cup, yet somehow still managing to look like a lady. Who would guess, moments earlier, she'd been a whirl of sharp fingernails? She'd scratched a teller in the face, drawing blood. She'd had to be held back, or she might've done worse.

Later, Pauline examines the bank statements. She'd been so

busy tidying up her father's bills and gathering his investments she hadn't looked closely at their joint account. It started when her father went into hospice. Every few days, someone took out cash, sometimes hundreds of dollars. But the incident with the bank seems to be the only time her mother tried to take out money after Emma moved in.

When Pauline and her mother return, Emma's in the foyer waiting. Pauline stands by, awkwardly watching her daughter take care of things. Emma eases Mrs. Shaw out of her trench coat, takes her by the elbow, and guides her into the warm house.

"Have a rest, Grandma," says Emma. "If you like, take your milk and settle yourself at the table. Dinner will be served in a few minutes."

Pauline's mother staggers towards the dining room, slopping milk.

Emma returns to the kitchen. "What'd they do to poor Grandma?" she whispers.

"Poor Grandma? You can't be serious. Your poor Grandma attacked a clerk at the bank. We're lucky they didn't press charges. She left scratch marks on the man's face."

"I should've kept her nails shorter. She was only sitting on the garden bench in the backyard. She's done that plenty of times, nothing bad ever happened. I only left her five minutes. I thought the fresh air would be good for her."

"Honey, it's nothing you did. It's nothing any of us have done, although we're paying for it. You should be in school, and I can't keep missing work."

Emma wipes her eyes and refastens her ponytail tighter than before. "Leave if you have to. I'll handle things here."

If Pauline doesn't do something, her daughter is going to keep throwing herself into the same unforgiving situation. The sun will go down. None of them can stop it. The illness is only going to get worse.

"It's time we put her in care. We can't put it off a day longer. That's final."

Pauline finds it surprisingly easy to evacuate her mother. Emma puts up such a fuss that Pauline has to trick her, but her mother never shows the least bit of resistance, at least not when she is being removed from the house.

After the lights go out in Emma's room, Pauline slips through the front door and creeps through the house.

She finds her mother in bed, patting the pillow in the empty space next to her. Her mother is humming, "Fly Me to the Moon." In a blinding moment of hope, Pauline almost kisses her wrinkly forehead and tells her to have a nice sleep.

Her mother has been growing more confused. Maybe that's why she does as she's told when Pauline leans towards her and says it's time to get dressed. Her mother and father always had season tickets to the symphony. Pauline tells her mother they're going to an evening of Gershwin. In the past, her mother would've worn a simple black dress with pearls, but she puts on orange pants and a pink shirt. And by the time they've driven across town and arrived at the manor, her mother has forgotten where they're supposed to be going.

The staff are pleased to accommodate the late arrival. The place looks more like a five-star hotel than an advanced care residence. The lobby is filled with wingback chairs and elegant maple side tables. The wide hallways have thick carpeting, and the walls are adorned with original art.

A personal care worker is standing by even though it's two o'clock in the morning. Pauline is not surprised that her parent's money pays for lots of services.

The personal care worker has a bad perm and a mouth that means business. "Take it easy, Mrs. Shaw," she says, guiding Pauline's mother by the arm down the hall.

Mrs. Shaw is given a room all her own, a studio apartment really, with a bedroom, sitting area and a kitchenette that's only for making tea because it doesn't have a stove. Staff will come once a week to clean the bathroom and the rest of the place. Three times a day, they will serve delicious gourmet meals.

Once inside the suite, the care worker deposits Pauline's mother into a brand-new lift chair. "Now, isn't that better, Mrs. Shaw? Rest a bit. We'll have you settled into a nice warm bed soon."

It's probably the lift chair that sets her off. Back home, Pauline's mother sat in the same red wingback chair she'd always used. The minute her back presses against the ugly grey lift chair, Mrs. Shaw's leg strikes out, her sharp-toed shoe stabbing the care worker's crotch.

"You are not my girl. Where's my sweet girl? What have you done to her?"

By the next day, Emma is also settled into the tiny suite meant for one. It's agreed that she'll stay one week at most, but after that, she's going back to her studies. Now that the hardest choice has been made, Emma seems willing to be reasonable.

But two months later, Emma is still there. Pauline visits as much as she can. She knows she should show up more often. Twilight has darkened the present moment, insisting on its forward momentum into oblivion, trapping all of them in a confusion of light that is neither bright nor dark.

When Pauline steps into the suite, her mother is stationed in her lift chair, a green plaid afghan over her lap. A glass of water rests on the over-bed table at her side. Her mother's face is slack, the mouth sloppy, and the eyes gazing at nothing. Since moving to the place where they're supposed to give memory extra care, her mother has deteriorated rapidly.

Pauline sets the shoebox on the small table in the kitchenette. She can talk to Emma about the contents later when the time seems right. They've all learned to assess her mother's condition before introducing something new. Pauline used the shoebox to collect the money hidden throughout the house. She didn't feel safe carrying all that cash, but she wanted to see her mother's face. How will her mother feel when she sees all that money? And Pauline will give it to her—nearly $8,000 in total.

Her mother is taking long breaths, in and out through the nose, a faint wheeze followed by a louder huff. Pauline touches the back of her mother's hand, feels the bluntness of the knuckles and the loose dry skin. When her mother shows no sign of having been touched, Pauline increases the pressure a little, one squeeze with a quick release. Her mother flinches, taking away her hand, hiding it under the afghan.

"Who let this woman into my room? Get her away from me." Pauline's mother still has a thick head of hair. A silver strand is caught in the corner of her mouth like she's eating her own hair.

For all of Pauline's life, her mother has been an absence, evidence only of what is not there. Wherever her mother goes, she leaves behind a vacuum. Pauline does what she can to stay out of the vortex, keep a safe distance and protect herself. But even now, when she's well into her fifties, no longer a girl, and her mother is old and fragile of body and mind, Pauline still gets sucked into the abyss.

There is no escape from her mother's words. They echo in the hollow of Pauline's mind, a final answer to the dread she's carried in her stomach for as long as she can remember. All the years of hoping for a flash of her mother's attention, wanting only a minute and hating that want, wishing instead to be free and not care. And now, none of it matters.

After her mother doesn't recognize her, Pauline stays away for a week. She speaks every night to Emma on the phone to make sure everything is okay. That's what draws her back. They need to put the money in the bank where it'll be safe, but her mother thrashes her arms every time Emma tries to pry the shoebox out of her grasp. Pauline's mother has even taken to sleeping with that shoebox beside her in bed at night and carrying it around like a baby in her arms during the day.

Pauline suggests they grab the shoebox while her mother is

napping. Given her memory, it shouldn't be too hard to remove the source of upset. All they have to do is take the shoebox. If her mother doesn't see the shoebox around, she won't remember it exists.

Her mother is snoring when they creep towards the bed. Emma holds back the cover. Pauline reaches for the shoebox. Her mother's eyes snap open, and she grabs the shoebox before stepping out of bed.

"Pauline," she says in a crackly voice. Her confused gaze goes straight to Emma. "Keep that person away from me."

Pauline is not surprised to hear her daughter called that name. Emma warned her it'd been happening. Pauline wonders how her mother really feels, what she'd do if given the chance to change her life, what this dream she's concocted in the mixed-up synapses of her clogged-up brain means to the real world here and now.

Her mother slips into her bathrobe and saunters out of the bedroom with the shoebox tucked under her arm. She's found new grace since losing more memory. The movements have become languid, without restraint. Anyone might think her mother is sleepwalking.

Once seated at the small dining table, her mother starts unpacking the box and counting, muttering words that do not quite make sense, "One. Tooter. Three. Four. Five. Sexty."

Emma says, "Let me take care of this."

Her mother's eyes keep darting to the side as if she's expecting someone, as if she's afraid. She can only drop one stack of bills into the shoebox at a time. Her body no longer has the coordination. "Quick, help me!" she whispers.

Emma joins in. Soon, all the money is stashed away, and the lid is back on. But it is not enough.

Her mother keeps looking from side to side, making sure the coast is clear. Her scrawny arms reach across the table and drag the shoebox closer. She tries to tuck it under her bathrobe, except it's too big and looks ridiculous. Half the box is not covered.

Her silver head of hair sinks into her shoulders. "Pauline," she hisses. "Don't ever let him open that lid. Never. Ever. No matter what happens, never let him see what's inside."

An unprepared person would shake their head at the absurdity of the situation, but Emma knows what to do. In a panicky whisper, mirroring the frightened woman in front of her, Emma offers reassurance and lets it be known they're sharing whatever moment is happening.

"You don't want him to see what's in the box?"

A nod.

Emma leans closer. "What would happen if he looked inside?"

A huff. "He would see what I have ... and he would take it." A wrinkly hand reaches out and snatches the air. "All my life, he's been taking things from me. I've told you that before."

Emma does not glance away from the pained eyes she's been holding to hers. "What did he take?"

Silence swirls around the room, sucking in air and all the tiny particles. Her mother's mouth pinches. A minute longer and Pauline might have been dragged into the abyss.

And then everything slows down. The spinning stops. Her mother looks upward. The line of her jaw grows strong. Pain washes over her face, and she widens her mouth in a show of teeth, yellow and worn but still sharp. "My sweet little girl. She was my whole life . . . and he took her from me. I hate him."

Pauline's mother still cradles the shoebox in her arms and sleeps with it at night, but the bundles of cash have been replaced with photocopies of dollar bills. Before returning full-time to her studies, Emma picked out a caregiver. It's working out well. Pauline visits as often as she can.

Two days before Christmas, they book a private dining room at the manor. While staff members serve turkey dinner, the three generations of women sit at a massive table with silver utensils on a white tablecloth.

Emma has finished her thesis. Graduation is in the spring. As she eats her salad, she talks about her new position at the hospital. Pauline toasts her daughter. The three women raise their glasses, and as happens sometimes, Pauline's mother spills a little on her chin.

Emma is the first to push back her chair, but Pauline holds out her hand. "I'll take care of this," she says. With a crisp white napkin, Pauline wipes her mother's chin.

And they continue their meal.

ACKNOWLEDGMENTS

I am grateful to Wendy Atkinson, the new publisher at Ronsdale Press. From start to finish, she has been supportive, collaborative and fun. Thank you to Rosemary Nixon and Heather Tekavec for editing, Kevin Welsh for proofreading and Dorian Danielsen for the book cover. I am grateful also to August at *Carve Critiques* and Alyse at *Craft* magazine for helpful feedback on the final versions of "Secret Workings."

Anyone fortunate enough to come under the care of Stella Leventoyannis Harvey knows what a gift that is. A moving example, a kind coach, a keen critic, and, above all, a community builder. I am grateful for her mentorship. As this collection began to get underway, Barbara Joan Scott helped me develop a sound foundation in the importance of complex characters. I am grateful for her support over the years and her razor-sharp eyes. When I was just beginning, I was lucky to have Lori Hahnel, courtesy of the Writers' Guild of Alberta Apprenticeship Program, work with me as I struggled to understand the short story form.

I began to find my voice when I immersed myself in a diverse writing community. Thank you, thank you, thank you to The Writer's Studio at Simon Fraser University. Sincere gratitude to my

2018 workshop group: K.J., Nicole, Paula, Sriram and Sabyasachi. Thank you also to the workshop group of 2019: Beth, Heige, Jeff, Isabella, Jenn, Joanna, Karen, Montana and Purnima. I learned so much from being your teacher's assistant.

In the neighbourhood where I live, my writing home is with the For the Love of Words (aka FLOW) crowd, who meet the last Tuesday of every month at the glorious Duncan Showroom to share words. Thank you, Longevity John and Bill, for making this truly open space. Appreciation also to Dr. Ted for high-quality sound. Not the least, I am grateful to all the good people who share themselves on that stage and listen as others do the same.

These stories benefitted from feedback given through blue pencil cafes, writer-in-residence programs and other means. Thank you to Angela Rydell, Barb Howard, Darrel McCleod, Deborah Willis and Jennifer Manuel. Warm gratitude to Rona Altrows, editor of the *You Look Good for Your Age* anthology, for her generosity, wisdom and talent for bringing writers together in full force.

I am grateful also to the more than twenty writers who agreed to be interviewed by me for *The Artisanal Writer*. Your insights on craft brought into question many notions I'd held about how to write fiction, which opened the door to fresh growth for me as a writer and a human being.

Sometimes the only way to get a true sense of things is to ask people with lived experience. Gratitude to Annky, Nancy and Pam for their generous help. Brenda gave her time to edit the submission manuscript. Really, so many people have been kind and supportive. If you're not mentioned, it's my memory and not the value of your contribution.

Over the years, certain people's lives have interwoven with mine, lending meaning and connection, and the sharing of both sorrow and joy. Other souls seem to magically appear in moments of suffering to offer comfort. Thank you Barb, Doug, Philip, Shanna, Shannon, Tracy and Wendy. As I was working on these stories, your presence helped me keep an open heart.

My sons have steadfastly believed that one day a book of mine would be published. Heck, Simon still thinks I'm going to be on *Oprah*. Donald has edited more versions of these stories than anyone should have to, always adding his honest reactions to the corrections. And Chris often talked to me about the urge to write and how it feels to imagine other people's lives. Writing is fulfilling, but it does not come close to the experience of being their mother.

He has cried with me. He has jumped up and down and danced around the kitchen with me. He is my first reader. More times than not, if I have a problem with a particular story, we will have a conversation, and he will say that one thing that cracks everything open. I love you, Greg. The adventure continues.

And finally, thank you, Frank, for suggesting twenty years ago that I should write a novel. I am pretty sure this is not what you had in mind, but your faith in me gave me the courage to start.

PREVIOUS PUBLICATIONS

Earlier versions of the following short stories were previously published in literary magazines and an anthology. Thank you to the editors.

"Intimacy." 2020. *Descant* 59.
"Secret Workings." 2021. *Phoebe*, 50, no 1.
"Sundowning." 2021. *You Look Good For Your Age*, edited by R. Altrows. Edmonton: University of Alberta Press.
"The Art of the Scarf." 2021. *You Look Good for Your Age*, edited by R. Altrows. Edmonton: University of Alberta Press.
"The Point of Failure." 2019. *Qwerty* 40.
"Your Body Was Made for This" (excerpt). 2018. *Emerge* 18.

SUPPLEMENTAL READING

As I was writing this collection, the following sources were particularly formative. Thank you to these authors and all the people who put human experience into words. This is how we glimpse each other and ourselves.

Allen, K. 2019. *Our Past Matters: Stories of Gay Calgary*. South Wales: AS-Publishing.

Braid, K. 2012. *Journeywoman: Swinging a Hammer in a Man's World*. Halfmoon Bay, BC: Caitlin Press.

Feil, N. 2002. *The Validation Breakthrough*. Baltimore: Health Professionals Press.

Gibson, L.C. 2015. *Adult Children of Emotionally Immature Parents*. Oakland, CA: New Harbinger Publications.

Graefe, S. (Ed.). 2018. *Swelling with Pride: Queer Conception and Adoption Stories*. Halfmoon Bay, BC: Caitlin Press.

Kessler, L. 2007. *Dancing with Rose: Finding Life in the Land of Alzheimer: One Daughter's Hopeful Story*. Toronto: Penguin Books.

Lewis, C.S. 2009. *A Grief Observed*. San Francisco: HarperOne.

Martin, E. 2001. *The Woman in the Body: A Cultural Analysis of Reproduction*. Boston: Beacon Press.

Noakes, T. 2003. *The Lore of Running*. Windsor, ON: Human Kinetics.

Perel, E. 2018. *The State of Affairs: Rethinking Infidelity*. San Francisco: Harper Paperbacks.

Schorn, S. 2013. *Smile at Strangers: And Other Lessons in the Art of Living Fearlessly*. Boston: Houghton Mifflin Harcourt.

Steinke, D. 2019. *Flash Count Diary: Menopause and the Vindication of Natural Life*. New York: Sarah Crichton Books.

ABOUT THE AUTHOR

Debbie Bateman is a graduate of The Writer's Studio at Simon Fraser University. Her short stories have appeared in literary journals and an anthology. Now a post-menopausal woman, she is too young to be told what she cannot do and old enough to know that most of us are a beautiful mess. She is a quiet rebel and a known troublemaker, a hugger of trees and a peaceful soul, and a practitioner of Buddhism. A proud mother of three sons, she lives in Quw'utsun (Cowichan) on Vancouver Island with her husband. She blogs about writing at debbiebateman.ca.